ALMOST LIKE LOVE

BOOKS BY ABIGAIL STROM

The Millionaire's Wish

Cross My Heart

Waiting for You

Into Your Arms

Winning the Right Brother

Almost Like Love

ALMOST LIKE LOVE

Abigail Strom

This is a work of fiction. Names, characters, organizations, places, events, and incidents are either products of the author's imagination or are used fictitiously.

Text copyright © 2014 Abigail Strom
All rights reserved.

No part of this book may be reproduced, or stored in a retrieval system, or transmitted in any form or by any means, electronic, mechanical, photocopying, recording, or otherwise, without express written permission of the publisher.

Published by Montlake Romance, Seattle

www.apub.com

Amazon, the Amazon logo, and Montlake Romance are trademarks of Amazon.com, Inc., or its affiliates.

ISBN-13: 9781477825884
ISBN-10: 1477825886

Cover design by Mary Anne Smith

Library of Congress Control Number: 2014940350

Printed in the United States of America

For Mikel and Owen, my favorite geeks

Chapter One

"This was a mistake."

As Kate Meredith stared at the East Village club from inside the taxi, her courage evaporated. She glanced down at herself and cringed at the sight of the bare skin Simone had insisted she put on display.

How had she let her friend talk her into this outfit? A leather miniskirt and a *bustier*, for God's sake. A bustier that, by the feel of it, had been designed by the Marquis de Sade out of black lace and agony.

At least she didn't have to worry about humiliating herself inside the club. She'd never make it that far on the four-inch heels Simone had convinced her to wear. The minute she stepped onto the sidewalk, she'd fall flat on her face.

"This is *not* a mistake," Simone said firmly. "As far as I'm concerned, this is the first rational thing you've done in years."

Kate turned her head to glare at her friend, who didn't look like a poster child for rationality at the moment. She was wearing a dress made of canary-yellow plastic, along with fishnet stockings and combat boots, and her short black hair was spiked with a product that had turned her normally silky locks into lethal weapons.

"This is your world, not mine," Kate said, turning back to look at the line of people waiting to get into the club. "I don't belong here. I look like a kid playing dress-up. Why did I let you—"

"The only thing I did wrong was failing to pour whiskey down your throat before we came here. Let's go rectify that now, shall we?"

Simone reached across her to open the cab door and then practically shoved Kate out onto the sidewalk. Kate teetered on her heels but didn't actually fall, and by the time Simone paid the driver and came to stand beside her, she was reasonably confident she could keep from face-planting on the asphalt.

While she was standing, anyway. She wasn't so sure about walking. And as for *dancing* . . .

She gripped Simone's shoulder. "Not my world," she said again.

"May I remind you that your world kicked your ass today? That's why you came to me, remember?"

It was true.

Kate had woken up that morning with a job and a fiancé. Eight hours later, she'd lost both of them.

So she could plead temporary insanity, couldn't she? Why else would she have pounded on Simone's door and announced that the two of them were going shopping—and then clubbing? She never went clubbing with Simone. She loved her friend like a sister, but they had very different ideas of what constituted a fun Friday night.

"I was obviously out of my mind. It was your job to talk me down off the ledge, not hand me a cape and tell me I could fly."

Simone laughed and put an arm around her waist. Since Kate was towering over her even more than usual, the hug brought Simone's face into contact with her left boob.

Simone took a step back and studied Kate's cleavage with satisfaction. "Your tits are *awesome* in that. If I ever get implants, this is what I want them to look like."

Kate wriggled her shoulders in an effort to relieve some of the pressure on her C cups, which, ratcheted up by the bustier, now resembled double Ds.

"I can't take a deep breath in this thing. And it's digging into me."

"No beauty without pain. I'm sweating like a pig in this dress, but do you hear me complaining? No, you do not."

Kate sighed and smoothed her hands over her hips. "I'm sweating, too, and it's not even summer yet. Okay, you know what? I've completely satisfied my urge to cut loose. Mission accomplished. I think it's time to go home now. I think I—"

The theme song from *Doctor Who* played inside her purse. Someone was calling her.

It was Chris. It had to be. He wanted to tell her he'd made a huge mistake—that he loved her, missed her, couldn't live without her.

"Hello?" she said breathlessly, not even bothering to check the caller ID after she fished the phone out of her purse.

"Kate! Oh, sweetie, how are you doing?"

Not Chris. Jessica.

Jessica, who was getting married in June. Jessica, who'd roomed with her and Simone in college and had asked them to be bridesmaids. Jessica, who'd once christened her Little Miss Boring after Kate had stayed in their dorm to watch the series finale of *Battlestar Galactica* instead of going to a frat party.

Kate sighed. "I'm fine, Jess. What do you need?" Jessica never hesitated to make use of her many bridesmaids for wedding-related tasks, and even though it was ten o'clock at night, that was no doubt the reason she was calling now.

"What do *I* need? Don't be silly. You can't think I'd be so cruel as to ask you for a favor when your heart is breaking."

Oh, great. Who'd told Jessica about—

"Tom and I ran into Chris tonight, and he told us what happened. He asked if he could bring Anastasia to the wedding."

Anastasia? Her name was *Anastasia*? No wonder Chris hadn't mentioned it when he'd announced that he'd fallen in love with another woman.

"Tom said yes before I could say a word. But after we left the restaurant, I made him promise that if you have a problem with it, we'll tell Chris he can't bring her. After all, you're in the wedding party—and I've known you longer than he's known Chris."

Kate's hand tightened around the phone. There was a roaring in her ears—the sound of a dam breaking, or possibly her head exploding.

"Of course I don't have a problem with it."

Her voice was eerily calm. Reasonable. Sweet, even.

"Oh, Kate—you're so brave! And don't worry. We have plenty of time before the wedding to scrounge up a date for you. You won't have to face Chris alone."

Jessica was going to *scrounge up* a date for her?

The roaring grew loader.

"You don't have to do that. I already have a date."

Her mouth, apparently, had decided to lead its own life.

"You *do*? Who is it?"

"No one you know," Kate said quickly. "He's, um, a rebound fling."

"A *rebound* fling? *You're* having a rebound fling? What's he like?"

An excellent question.

"Well, uh . . . he's not much in the brains department, but he's amazing in bed."

"You've had *sex* already?"

Considering that Kate had had sex with exactly three men in her life and had been single today for a total of six hours, Jessica had some reason to sound stunned.

"Yep. Lots and lots of sex. Actually, I think that's him at the door. He must be back for a"—what was the phrase?—"booty call. So I'll talk to you later, okay?"

She stuffed the phone back into her purse and took a deep breath. For the first time tonight, she no longer felt like an awkward giant beside her petite friend. She felt like a Valkyrie. Like Athena going into battle. Like . . .

Simone was grinning at her. "You're having a rebound fling with a fictional guy?"

"He won't be fictional for long."

Her friend raised an eyebrow. "Really. And where are you planning to find him?"

Kate nodded towards the club. "In there."

Simone looked skeptical. "I don't think the men in there are your type."

"Exactly. I'm sick of my type. I'm sick of people like Jessica assuming I'll sit in my apartment and cry over Chris until her wedding, which I'll be forced to go to alone because I couldn't *scrounge up* a date. I'm sick of... I'm sick of..."

And suddenly it came out—the truth that had been bubbling up inside her since the network cancelled her show and her fiancé cancelled their relationship.

"I'm sick of *myself*. I'm sick of being the well-meaning idiot everyone feels sorry for. I'm sick of always trying to do the right thing and always getting screwed. I'm sick of thinking about everyone but me."

The bustier didn't seem so painful as reckless courage swept through her. "From this moment forward, I'm going to be a selfish bitch. I'm going into that club to find a man with tattoos and piercings and bad news written all over him. I'm going to bring him to Jessica's wedding and make Chris Corrigan eat his cheating heart out. I'm going to use him for sex, and then I'm going to dump him. Ruthlessly."

"Ruthlessly?"

"Ruthlessly."

Simone patted her shoulder. "Okeydokey. Let's go find you a rebound fling."

Kate's newfound confidence faltered for a moment. "Can we have a drink first?"

"Absolutely. Many, many, many drinks."

Ian Hart didn't usually spend his Friday nights in East Village clubs, or any club, for that matter. His partying days had been over for a long time. And even if he did want to go out, he wouldn't have gone tonight. He was in a lousy mood, and he'd give anything to be home right now, going over last week's ratings and financial reports.

Unfortunately, this was a special occasion. Mick Kalen, one of his oldest friends, was getting married tomorrow, and this was where the best man had decided to hold the bachelor party.

So Ian had gotten a babysitter for his nephew, dug out a pair of jeans from the back of his closet, and put on his old leather jacket over a long-sleeved shirt. Now he was sitting at a big round table covered with shot glasses, wondering exactly how much Wild Turkey it would take for him to go from pretending to have a good time to actually having a good time.

"All right, Mick. Pick out the hottest girl in here, and I'll get her for you."

That was Arthur, the groom's brother and best man.

Mick grinned at him. "How are you planning to do that? And what's going to happen if you do get her? This isn't a strip club, man. I don't think one of the women in here is going to give me a lap dance."

"It's not my fault you refused to go to the Foxy Lady."

"Not my scene."

"I know, I know. But can you at least flirt with a hot chick on your last night of freedom? Since you refuse to even get wasted."

"I don't want to be hungover on my wedding day. But I'll tell you what—I'll pick out a girl, and if you can talk her into coming over here, I'll flirt with her."

Out of the seven men sitting around the table, Arthur probably had the least chance of persuading a woman to do anything.

He wasn't bad looking, but he had one of the worst pickup track records of anyone Ian knew. He tried to start conversations about obscure comic books and science fiction shows, and although there were probably a few women in the world who would respond to that approach, you didn't often find them in the strip clubs or trendy bars where Arthur usually tried to make his move.

After a moment, Mick pointed across the room. "Okay, that one. The redhead at the bar."

The guys sitting on Mick's side of the table whistled, but by the time Ian twisted his head to look, the woman was facing away from them, leaning forward to say something to the bartender.

He couldn't see her face, but the rear view was definitely worth a second look. Lustrous red hair tumbled down her back, and her body was incredible, showcased by a tiny leather skirt and a strapless top that laced up in the back like a corset. The outfit made her look like a va-va-voom Hollywood starlet with hourglass curves and legs a mile long.

"I have the perfect opening line," Arthur announced.

"Yeah? What is it?" Mick asked.

"She looks exactly like Red Sonja."

"Who?"

The question came from several of the guys around the table, but Arthur didn't hear it. He was already gone, heading towards the curvaceous redhead with the confident swagger he always used when he approached a woman.

"Who said this bachelor party wouldn't have entertainment?" Mick said, leaning back in his chair to watch his brother's progress around the edge of the dance floor.

"Who the hell is Red Sonja?" Ian asked, unable to take his eyes off of whatever was about to happen. It was like driving in a snowstorm and seeing a car go into a slow skid, heading towards an inevitable collision.

"*Star Wars* or *Star Trek* character is my guess," Gabe Myers said, before tossing back a shot.

"That's a safe bet," Mick agreed. "This should be good."

Ian debated the wisdom of having another shot himself. Just as he'd decided against it, Gabe slid one in front of him.

"Go for it," his friend said. "You need something to cheer you up."

Ian frowned. "Who says I'm not cheery?"

"Even the prospect of watching Arthur crash and burn in truly spectacular fashion hasn't lifted you out of the pit of gloom you showed up here in. Did you have a bad day, or what?"

In spite of himself, Ian flashed back to the image he'd spent the last eight hours trying to forget—Kate Meredith waiting for the elevator, her arms around a cardboard box of her belongings.

When their eyes met, her expression went from forlorn to scathing in the blink of an eye. Then the elevator doors opened and she stepped inside before he could say a word.

Not that there'd been anything to say.

"I'm sorry I cancelled your show."

That would have gone over big. And why the hell should *he* apologize because *her* ratings were lousy? He was the VP of programming, not a guidance counselor.

That was the problem with creative types. They thought they could sit in their ivory towers and make things up while someone else took care of the rest. They didn't understand that no one was entitled to a living. That everything was a struggle. That you had to fight and claw your way to success.

Kate always acted like she was above all that. She hated talking about ratings and ad revenue and all the practical aspects of running a television network. And in the end, her distaste for the financial side of her business had cost her. It wasn't enough that she had written a good children's television show—and *Life with Max* was good, Ian couldn't deny that. His nephew loved it. But that didn't mean—

Arthur came up beside the curvy redhead and said something. She turned her head, and Ian got his first glimpse of her face.

Kate Meredith.

The curvy redhead was *Kate Meredith*.

It couldn't be . . . but it was.

The Kate Meredith he knew never wore heels, or makeup, or even skirts. She didn't give a damn about her appearance, which was one of the many things he found annoying about her. Your appearance sends a message to people, and you should always do everything in your power to make sure you send the right message.

But Kate couldn't be bothered to care about that. She was oblivious to it all, drifting happily along in her fantasy world where heroes and heroines were real, substance mattered more than form, and good triumphed over evil.

Unlike most women in the entertainment industry, Kate never used her appearance as a weapon. She downplayed her height, her hair, her face . . . and her body. Even at network parties and awards shows, Kate dressed to blend into the background rather than stand out.

Of course, she hadn't been able to disguise herself completely. Even in her dowdy work clothes, it had been obvious that Kate was attractive—and that she had the potential to be a lot more.

Ian had wondered more than once what it would take to make Kate cut loose. Apparently, losing her job had done the trick.

A rush of attraction was followed by a wave of guilt. It was hard to say which feeling he resented more.

She looked incredible. She was tall to begin with, but her high heels made her an Amazon. Her hair was a tumbled mass of red glory. And her body . . .

Sweet holy Christ.

She was stunning. She was every man's fantasy. She was . . .

Talking to Arthur Kalen.

Of course she was. There was probably one woman in ten thousand who would actually respond to Arthur's pickup approach, and Kate Meredith was it. She was a nerd, just like him—only it turned out she was trapped in the body of a sex goddess.

She was laughing at something Arthur had said. The bartender set a shot in front of her and she tossed it off, looking pretty damn sexy until a fit of coughing ruined the effect. Arthur got her a drink of water and patted her on the back.

Kate didn't usually drink—Ian knew that from seeing her at parties and red-carpet events. The alcohol she was downing now had to be hitting her like a ton of bricks.

Arthur was looking ecstatic, as well he might. Heaven had answered his prayers. Kate Meredith was everything he'd ever dreamed of—a beautiful, sexy geek on her way to being drunk off her ass.

Ian shoved his chair back and got to his feet. He couldn't let this happen. It was his fault that Kate had temporarily lost her mind, his fault that she'd gone out to drown her troubles dressed like an extra from *Showgirls*.

"Where are you going?"

He glanced down at Gabe. "I know that woman. I've got to rescue her from Arthur."

"Rescue her from *Arthur*? There's not a woman alive who needs to be rescued from Arthur. He's harmless."

Compared with most men, maybe he was. But the bar for decent behavior among his gender was set pretty low. And no man alive would be able to resist the chance to go home with that woman.

Which meant she did need rescuing. And in spite of the fact that he was probably the last man on earth Kate Meredith wanted to see right now, Ian was going to rescue her.

∽

Simone came off the dance floor looking sweaty and happy.

"Who's your friend?" she asked, noticing Comic Book Guy.

"The man who just gave me the single greatest compliment I have ever received."

"Wow. What was it?"

"He said I look like Red Sonja."

Simone looked perplexed for a moment. "Who—oh. She's one of the superhero chicks you have framed on your wall, right? The one who fights with the guy whose name sounds like a late-night talk-show host?"

"Conan the Barbarian."

"That's it." Simone cast the appraising glance of a costume designer over Kate. "You know, he has a point. All we have to do is dress you up with a sword and a barbed-wire bikini."

"I'd pay to see that," Comic Book Guy said, looking a little dazed. He wasn't at all what Kate was looking for tonight, but he was a nice guy and his flattery was a welcome balm after Chris's betrayal.

Simone waved the bartender over. "I'll buy the next round. What are you drinking?"

"The blood of my enemies," Kate said, causing Comic Book Guy to burst out laughing.

"Nothing for me," he said to Simone. "I'm going to the men's room. Do you promise you'll still be here when I come back?" he asked Kate.

"Sure."

Simone shook her head as he walked off towards the restrooms. "I can't believe you managed to meld with the geek hive-mind here. I thought we were supposed to be visiting *my* world tonight. This is more like that time you made me go to Comic-Con."

Kate patted her shoulder. "Comic-Con wasn't so bad. You said you got some great costume ideas there."

"I also got propositioned by some very weird people."

"You get propositioned everywhere."

Simone grinned at her. "Tonight I think you're the one who's going to get—"

She stopped short, staring at something over Kate's right shoulder. Wondering if Comic Book Guy had changed his mind about the bathroom break, Kate turned her head to look behind her.

For a moment she thought she was seeing things. She didn't usually drink hard liquor—maybe the alcohol in her system was making her hallucinate. Why else would she be seeing Ian Hart, the man responsible for cancelling her show? The universe couldn't be so perverse as to put her face-to-face with her archnemesis tonight, could it?

"Kate," he said, and she was forced to acknowledge that this was reality.

"I don't like you," she heard herself say.

Damn. She should have gone with something much stronger. Something like, "I'm going to reach down your throat, pull out your beating heart, and feed it to my cat." That's what Red Sonja would say.

Or would if she had cats, which she probably didn't.

Ian winced. "I know I'm not your favorite person right now."

"You should be her favorite person," Simone said, sliding off her barstool. "You're my favorite person, and I don't even know you."

Kate glared at her. "Simone, this is Ian Hart."

Her friend's eyes widened. "The evil bastard with no soul?"

"In the flesh."

Simone looked him over. "I was picturing someone less . . . yummy."

"The devil comes disguised as a gorgeous man."

Ian's eyebrows went up, and she could have kicked herself. She'd meant to insult him, and instead she'd called him gorgeous. Which he was, unfortunately. It was one of the most annoying things about him.

She could still remember the first time she'd seen him, almost two years ago now. In the blissful minutes before she'd known who he was, she'd figured he had to be an actor, even though he was dressed like a corporate suit.

He was too good-looking to be anything else. He was well over six feet tall and had a perfect body, but it was his face that made a woman struggle not to drool. Rugged features framed by dark hair, and a smile that—

A smile that concealed a microscopic heart. Ian put a price tag on everything, and the only value he recognized was monetary. In Kate's eyes, he was the very definition of evil.

It wasn't fair that a man she despised so much should be so damn hot.

He looked even hotter than usual tonight, curse him. She'd never seen him dressed so casually before. He was wearing jeans and a worn leather jacket, and with his dark hair all tousled and a little rough stubble on his jaw, he looked good enough to eat.

The smug, insufferable bastard.

She folded her arms. "Go away, Hart. I'm trying to enjoy myself."

He sighed. "I know you're not thrilled to see me, Kate. But I came over here with good intentions."

"Really."

"Yeah. I'm not going to let you make a stupid mistake just because you had a bad day."

For the first time since he'd come over here, his eyes dropped to her cleavage. It was only a second before his eyes were riveted to her face again, but a flash of heat went from her toes to the top of her head.

She was more than a little tipsy, and she'd been concentrating on a) not punching Ian in the face and b) not letting him know she thought he was sexy. Because of that, she'd actually forgotten what she herself was wearing.

What must Ian be thinking right now?

Not that she gave a damn what he thought. Red Sonja never had any qualms about putting herself out there, did she? She used her unique fashion sense to say to the world, *This is my body. I use it to crush my foes.*

Instead of hunching her shoulders or slouching down, Kate stood up straighter. In her heels she was almost eye to eye with this particular foe.

"I didn't have a bad day, Hart. I had an apocalyptic day. The kind of day that entitles a woman to make a stupid mistake." She paused a moment. "Just to clarify, though—what stupid mistake are we talking about?"

"Going home with Arthur."

"Arthur? Who's Arthur?"

"The guy you were just talking to."

Comic Book Guy?

Kate shook her head vigorously. "No, no, no. I'm not going home with him. He's great, but we have too much in common. And he's too sweet."

Ian stared at her. "Too *sweet*?"

"Absolutely. I'm here to find a bad boy. Trouble with a capital *T*. A sex god who's great in bed and has no other redeeming qualities. Someone completely different from my—"

She stopped. There was no need to let him in on the other half of her rotten day. The last thing she needed was whatever passed as pity or sympathy from Ian Hart.

Unfortunately, Simone hadn't gotten that memo.

"Someone different from her fiancé," she finished helpfully. "He broke off their engagement today, the asshole. Between that and losing her job, Kate needed a good time tonight. So here we are."

Kate steeled herself to meet Ian's eyes, and there it was: pity. But for some reason, she wasn't as irritated by the expression as she'd expected to be. It made him look almost human. Like his calcified heart was experiencing an actual emotion.

"Jesus. I'm sorry, Kate. That really sucks."

He rubbed a hand across his jaw, which drew Kate's attention to the stubble there. A woman who kissed that face would have whisker burn for days. Every time she looked in the mirror, she'd think of him.

He slid his hands into his pockets. "Okay, so you didn't have a run-of-the-mill bad day. I get that. But you still shouldn't do something you'll regret tonight. Especially when you've been drinking."

She forced herself to focus on his words and not his mouth. It was much easier to hate him that way. "Wow. How condescending, Hart. Maybe if you try really hard you could be even more paternalistic."

The sympathy in his eyes was replaced by irritation, an expression she was much more used to seeing when Ian looked at her.

"You are the most annoying woman alive. You know that? For once, can't you just—"

"Hey, man, what are you doing here?"

Comic Book Guy—Arthur—had come back from the bathroom. He didn't look particularly pleased to see Ian.

"He's here to rescue me," Kate told him. "He's afraid you're going to take advantage of me in my drunken state."

Ian glared at her before turning to Arthur. "I don't think you're going to take advantage of her. But I know this woman, and she's not in great shape right now. She lost her job and her fiancé today. She's vulnerable."

The son of a bitch. "I lost my job because of *you*." She took a deep breath. "Okay, that's it. I'm going to do it. I've always wanted to, and now I am."

Ian looked at her again. "Do what?"

"Punch you in the face."

Of course she wouldn't really hit him—probably. She just meant to threaten him with her Red Sonja fist of fury.

But Simone grabbed her arm as she raised it. "Whoa there, cowgirl. I know we're supposed to be cutting loose tonight, but let's not get arrested for assault this early, okay? Let's save that for the wee hours."

"Spoilsport," Kate grumbled.

Still, she supposed her friend had a point. Ian was just the kind of guy who'd call the cops on her for taking a swing at him.

She folded her arms again. "Okay, fine. Here's what's going to happen. Arthur's going to give me his number, because I'd like to get together with him sometime to talk about comic books. Then the two of you are going back to wherever you came from so I can get on with my mission."

Ian had his poker face on. "Finding a bad boy, you mean."

"That's right."

Arthur looked from one of them to the other. "Kate may or may not be drunk, but I definitely am. Too drunk to follow this conversation, anyway. But I like the part about us getting together sometime," he added with a quick grin, fishing a business card out of his wallet and handing it to her. "My cell number's on the back. Call me anytime."

He clapped Ian on the shoulder. "See you back at the table, buddy."

Kate watched him go. "He seems like a real player," she said sarcastically. "A seducer of thousands. Thank God you were here to save me."

The muscles in Ian's jaw tightened, and he didn't say anything for a moment. She wondered if he was counting to ten.

"Just tell me this, Kate. What are you really looking for tonight?"

"I told you. A bad boy."

Once again, Simone stepped into the breach. "Specifically, she wants a guy with tattoos and piercings and bad news written all over him. She's going to use him for sex and then dump him ruthlessly. Also, she's going to take him to this nightmare wedding we're both in, so she can make her cheating ex eat his heart out. He's going to be there with his new girlfriend."

"Her name is Anastasia," Kate muttered.

Ian looked at her for a moment, his expression hard to read. Then he shook his head. "What the hell kind of name is Anastasia?"

She felt an unexpected rush of gratitude. "My thoughts exactly," she said.

One corner of Ian's mouth—that sinfully mobile mouth—lifted in a smile.

"I tell you what," he said. "If I find you a bad boy who'll go to this wedding with you, will that be enough?"

She looked at him suspiciously. "Enough for what?"

"Enough to . . . satisfy you. Without sex," he added.

Kate blinked. Ian Hart was going to find her a bad boy? A bad boy who would take her to Jessica's wedding but wouldn't have sex with her?

"Is he gay?"

"No."

"Then why wouldn't he want to have sex? Are you saying a guy like that wouldn't be attracted to me? Are you saying I'm so boring I can't even—"

Ian held up a hand. "Hold it right there. Believe me when I tell you that every straight man in this place is attracted to you, Kate. But this particular man . . ." He hesitated. "Let's just say he's got a chivalrous side. He doesn't sleep with women under the influence. Not on the first date, anyway."

She frowned. "So he's a safe bad boy."

"Well . . . yeah. Kind of."

If a guy was safe or chivalrous or whatever, could he still qualify as a bad boy?

"Does he have tattoos? I'm not talking temporary."

"Yeah."

"Piercings?"

"Not a lot, but yeah."

What other fantasy elements had she been imagining?

"Does he drive a motorcycle?"

Ian grinned. "Yeah."

Ian's grin was rare, and, as always when she saw it, Kate's stomach did a little flip.

"I think you should take him up on the offer," Simone said suddenly. "With the proviso that the guy he's got in mind is sufficiently sexy," she added. "If not, then the deal's off."

"That's right," Kate agreed. "He's got to be smoking."

Ian grinned again. "I don't know what would qualify as smoking in your book, so how about this? If the guy doesn't meet your standards of sexiness, you can go back to your original plan and find one on your own."

"And you'll go away and stop bothering me?"

"Cross my heart."

With an odd feeling that she was stepping off the edge of a cliff, Kate nodded her head. "I guess it wouldn't hurt to take a look at him."

"Great. Wait right here, and he'll be over in a few minutes."

Kate and Simone watched him walk away, navigating through the crowd with his easy, loose-limbed stride.

"A safe bad boy," Kate said musingly. "Who do you think he has in mind? It's got to be a friend of his, right?"

"Maybe," Simone said. Her smile, when Kate glanced at her, was more catlike than usual.

"What?" she asked.

"Nothing."

Ian disappeared into the crowd. "What do you think this guy will be like?"

Simone shook her head. "I don't know," she said, hopping up on a barstool. "But personally, I can't wait to find out."

Chapter Two

He had to be out of his mind.

As Ian headed back to his table, he wondered what the hell he was doing. He couldn't blame the alcohol; it would take more than a few shots of Wild Turkey to affect his judgment this much.

He decided it was Kate's fault. She'd disabled half his brain cells with that damn outfit and exploded the rest by announcing her intention to find a bad boy to go home with.

Imagining her with Arthur had been bad enough. But she seemed determined to go looking for trouble tonight, and he knew from experience that if you go looking for trouble you'll usually find it.

And he couldn't let anything happen to Kate . . . not after the day she'd had.

Which meant he was stuck. And since the only way he could save her from herself was to produce a bad boy for her, he'd produce one.

Back at his table, he assessed the resources available to him.

Other than him, Gabe was the tallest guy here—and he was wearing a short-sleeved black tee. Perfect.

"I need to borrow your shirt," he said, pulling off his jacket and slinging it over the back of his chair.

Gabe stared at him. "Huh?"

"Your shirt. I need it. You can wear mine instead," he added.

Gabe frowned. "I'm wearing short sleeves. You never wear short sleeves."

"Yeah, I know. Special circumstances."

He checked to make sure Simone and Kate weren't looking this way and was relieved to see them engrossed in conversation at the bar.

"This is very weird," Gabe said, but he pulled off his shirt and handed it to Ian, who handed over his in exchange.

Gabe was narrower in the chest and shoulders than Ian was, so the black cotton was stretched a little tight. But he'd accomplished his goal: his tattoos were on full display, from his biceps down to his forearms.

Mick watched the wardrobe exchange with his eyebrows raised. "When did we take the time machine back to the nineties? I haven't seen those tats since high school. Not outside of the gym, anyway."

"Long story," Ian said, looking around for the next item on his list.

He grabbed a kid walking by. "I'll pay you a hundred bucks for"—he thought for a second—"three of your earrings."

He'd once sported a lot more piercings than that, but most of them had closed up over the years, leaving two in his left ear and one in his right that he could put a stud through without drawing blood.

The kid blinked. He was probably figuring he'd still have plenty of earrings left after giving up three, and a hundred bucks would buy a lot of beer.

"You got it," he said. "Which ones?"

Ian chose a black skull, a silver cross, and a fake-diamond stud. The kid took them out while Ian counted out five twenties.

Gabe picked up the jewelry from the table before Ian could.

"I don't think that guy has showered in a while. Let me sterilize these." He dropped them into a shot of vodka and pushed it towards Ian. "Okay, that should do it."

"Good thinking," Ian said, fishing out the earrings and putting them in.

All the guys at the table were staring at him now.

"What the hell?" asked Stephen.

"Long story," Ian said again. "By the way, can I borrow your Harley?"

"Hell, no, you can't borrow my—"

"Oh, let him have it," Mick interrupted. "You can go home in the limo with us. I don't know what's going on, but Ian's obviously on some kind of mission. Maybe he's going undercover for the CIA."

Stephen grumbled but gave in, fishing the keys out of his pocket and tossing them across the table.

"Just make sure you take care of my baby."

"You bet." Ian looked at Mick. "It's okay if I bail?"

"As long as you're at the church on time tomorrow. Good luck on your mission."

"Thanks, man."

On his way back to the bar, he stopped off at the men's room and took a look in the mirror.

He shook his head slowly. Was he really going out there like this? To help a woman who irritated him like a case of prickly heat and hated his guts into the bargain?

Oh, well, what the hell. Call it his good deed for the year.

Needing one more disreputable touch, he turned on the faucet and stuck his hands under the water for a second. Then he ran them through his hair, messing it up as much as he could.

It wasn't perfect, but at least he matched the earrings a little better now.

He grinned suddenly at his reflection. This wasn't the usual armor for a white knight doing his best to rescue a damsel in distress, but it would have to do.

Kate was tossing down her third shot of the night when Simone gave a sudden gasp.

"Sweet Mary and Joseph. If you don't want him, will you let me have him? Please?"

Kate spun her barstool around to look, and her brain short-circuited.

It was Ian Hart—in the same way that Clark Kent is Superman.

He was leaning against the bar with a half smile on his face. Kate took him in from his toes to the top of his head and gave a silent prayer of thanks that she was sitting down.

Whatever fantasy man she'd been picturing in her head, this one looked better.

The business suits Ian usually wore gave an impression of size and muscle while leaving something to the imagination. Kate realized now that Ian's secret identity as Corporate Guy had been protecting the women of Manhattan from the full effect of his sheer masculine power.

His chest and shoulders were a wall of muscle barely contained by the thin material of his tee shirt. His arms were covered in tattoos that extended to the middle of his forearms. The gleam of silver and onyx at his ears gave him the air of a pirate or a gangster, depending on your fancy. His black hair was rakishly disheveled and, along with the stubble on his jaw, presented a tactile temptation almost impossible to resist.

She curled her fingers into the palms of her hands so they wouldn't do anything of their own volition.

"So what's the verdict? Do I pass muster?"

Pass muster? Pass muster for what?

Oh, God—she'd completely forgotten what this was about.

She was supposed to be finding a bad boy to go with her to Jessica's wedding. Ian had offered to find one for her, and now he was standing there, looking like . . . that.

Simone poked her in the ribs. "What's the verdict, Kate?"

Her mouth had gone dry. "I . . . um . . ."

For the life of her, she couldn't think of a way to finish that sentence.

"You said your date for this wedding had to be smoking," Ian reminded her.

Her brain had forgotten how to form words. "Uh . . ."

He grinned at her, and an electric rush tightened the muscles low in her belly.

"You're absolutely right," he said, as though she'd produced a reasoned argument instead of a wordless mumble. "You can't be expected to make a decision without dancing with me first."

One of her hands was on the bar; the other was in her lap. He reached for the one on her lap.

"Let's go," he said, his warm, strong fingers closing over hers.

Before she knew what was happening, he'd pulled her off the barstool and was leading her towards the dance floor. She cast a panicked glance over her shoulder at Simone, who grinned and waved.

No help there.

He turned and stopped at the same time, and she bumped into that broad expanse of chest.

With the front of her bustier.

Heat flooded her face. "Oh my God, I'm so sorry. This thing makes me more, um, convex than usual."

"No problem," he said.

She risked a glance at him. He was looking at her with a curious kind of intentness, as though she were a knot he was trying to unravel.

"I didn't know your eyes were hazel," she heard herself say. "I always thought they were green. But they're hazel, aren't they? Did you know that hazel eyes are a combination of Rayleigh scattering, which is the same principle that makes the sky look blue, and melanin, which is the pigment that makes brown eyes brown?"

One corner of his mouth quirked up. "I did not, in fact, know that."

"Oh. Did you know—"

He put his hands on her waist and said her name. "Kate."

Between the bottom of her bustier and the top of her leather skirt was a strip of bare skin. It was there that Ian's palms settled, the contact sending warmth piercing through her like shafts of sunlight.

She forgot whatever she'd been about to say. "Yes?"

"To everything there is a season. A time to talk, and a time to dance. Right now it's time to give your incandescent verbal plumage a rest."

A well-turned phrase always got Kate's attention. "'Incandescent verbal plumage,'" she repeated. "That's good."

"Thank you. Now shut up."

If she couldn't talk, the only thing left to do was dance—and she hadn't been out dancing since college.

Where should she put her hands? And how much space could she leave between the two of them without looking like she was at a seventh-grade formal? She didn't want to risk another chest bump.

But the answers to those questions weren't left up to her.

Ian took her hands and lifted them to his shoulders. The action brought her flush against him, and a thousand tiny pinpricks shivered her skin.

When he put his hands back on her body, they went a little lower—to her hips instead of her waist.

Then he started to move.

Until that moment, she wouldn't have said there was anything particularly sexy about the music playing in the club, which was fast with a techno beat. But Ian picked up on the bass line underneath, and he translated that slower, sexier rhythm into the sway of their bodies.

In her high heels she was only an inch or so shorter than he was. They fit together with unexpected perfection, his rock-hard contours eliciting a subtle pliancy in her body.

There was an unfamiliar ache in her breasts. They felt heavy and soft and voluptuous, but at the same time her nipples hardened into tight little buds.

Could he feel that?

If she met his eyes, she might find out. She might see a satisfied smirk or a knowing grin.

So she didn't look at him. Instead, she closed her eyes and rested her head on his shoulder.

Mmmmmmm.

He smelled like clean male skin with a faint undernote of musk. She'd sat next to him at a meeting once and gotten a whiff of expensive cologne, but he wasn't wearing that tonight.

His shoulder was so broad and strong. She was a tall woman, but next to Ian she felt fragile and feminine—another unfamiliar sensation.

"Mmmmmmm."

Ian's hands tightened on her hips, and she realized she'd voiced her pleasure out loud this time.

Damn.

She held her breath and was relieved when he didn't say anything. But those big hands pulled her even closer, fitting her more securely against his body.

Her belly seemed to hollow out as honeyed warmth spread through her.

What was happening to her? Sure, she'd talked a good game about looking for a guy tonight . . . but she hadn't really expected to feel attracted to someone so soon after her fiancé dumped her.

And this was more than attraction. She was so turned on her hair might be standing on end.

Another thought clamored for attention in her pleasure-fogged brain. But how was she supposed to think straight when Ian had found that place on her waist again and was stroking it softly, his thumbs making lazy sweeps against her bare skin?

When rationality finally broke through, she had to force herself to lift her head from his shoulder.

"You cancelled my show," she blurted, hanging onto that fact as if it were a port in a storm.

His hands stilled, but he didn't let her go.

"I know," he said, the low timbre of his voice sending new darts of sensation through her.

"I don't like you."

"I know that, too."

"If I seem to be enjoying myself that's only because I'm drunk and . . . and . . ."

"Vulnerable," he suggested.

"Yes, vulnerable. Because you cancelled my show," she said again.

"Right. So that means I owe you."

He bent his head towards her as he spoke, and his jaw brushed against her cheek. She felt the scrape of rough stubble across her flushed skin.

She took a deep breath. "Absolutely. You owe me big."

The song ended. In the quiet before the next one began, Ian stepped back to look at her, putting a little space between them.

Kate had never been so relieved and so disappointed at the same time.

Those hazel eyes looked into hers. "So let me be your date to the wedding. I'll make your ex eat his heart out, and I'll make every other woman there wish she was you."

The wedding. She'd almost forgotten about it again.

For the first time, she imagined showing up at the Ritz-Carlton reception with Ian Hart on her arm. Whether he came as Corporate Guy or Tattooed Bad Boy, there was no question he'd be the smoking-hot date of her dreams.

Which was what she'd come here looking for. Right?

She was still having trouble thinking straight. She was also feeling a little . . . disheveled. She smoothed her hands down her leather skirt, making sure it hadn't ridden up her thighs, and then tucked her hair behind her ears.

Ian followed her movements with his eyes. His gaze warmed her skin as though he'd touched her.

She swallowed. "Okay, fine. You can take me to the wedding. It's on"—what the hell was the date?—"June twelfth." She remembered something else: "I may need you for the rehearsal dinner, too."

His eyes gleamed with something—satisfaction, or maybe amusement. Not that she cared what he was feeling, of course. She needed a hot date, and Ian Hart fit the bill. And since this was partial payback for his cancelling her show, it was kind of like a business transaction.

"I'll keep that weekend open," he said. "And now I have a favor to ask you."

She frowned. "You don't get to ask me a favor. You could take me to ten weddings and you'd still owe me." But then her curiosity got the better of her. "What is it?"

"I'd appreciate it if you'd let me take you home now."

Her frown deepened. "Now? I only got here an hour ago. What if I'm not ready to leave yet? And how is that a favor to you, anyway?"

One corner of his mouth lifted in a smile. "I'm afraid that if you stay, you'll keep drinking. And then you might find some other bad boy you like more than me."

She spoke without thinking. "I wouldn't—" She stopped herself just in time and coughed. "I wouldn't be surprised if I did," she finished primly.

His smile turned into a grin. "So why don't you let me take you home now? You drank, you danced, you hung out with your friend and got hit on by Arthur. That's pretty good for a night on the town. Why don't you cap it off with a ride on a motorcycle? That was one of your requirements for a bad boy, right?"

She stared at him. "You have a motorcycle?"

"I used to, a long time ago. I borrowed one tonight just for you."

He used to drive a motorcycle. Her gaze drifted down to the tattoos on his arms, and she wondered if they dated from the same period in his history.

She reached out and traced one of the tattoos with the tip of a finger. It was gorgeous—a red-and-black dragon twisting sinuously around Ian's bicep.

"How old were you when you got these?"

"Old enough to know better," he said after a moment. His voice sounded husky, and she looked at him.

Their eyes locked, and she lost track of the conversation. Then she snatched her hand away from his arm and cleared her throat.

"You don't have to drive me home. And you don't have to worry about me. I'll hang out with Simone a while longer and go home with her."

Ian looked over her shoulder, towards the bar. "Simone looks busy."

Kate turned her head and saw her friend chatting with a cute guy. "She's just passing the time. She wouldn't ditch me for a guy—not after the day I've had."

"If you go home with me, she won't have to make that choice." He paused for a second. "And by 'go home with me,' I mean let me drive you home and see you to your door."

She rolled her eyes. "I get that you're not propositioning me, Hart. You don't have to keep emphasizing it."

She glanced back at Simone again. As though he sensed that she was wavering, Ian's voice turned persuasive. "It's a Harley. Black leather, chrome, and more power than you've ever felt between your legs. A bad girl's dream. What do you say?"

A bad girl's dream.

She had no idea how he was doing it, but Ian seemed to know exactly what to say to her tonight.

"Okay, you've convinced me. I'll tell Simone I'm leaving and meet you out front in a few minutes."

As she made her way through the crowd, she replayed another choice phrase in her head.

More power than you've ever felt between your legs.

If any other man said that, she'd assume it was a come-on . . . or else that he was overcompensating for something.

But neither of those scenarios applied to Ian. He'd made it clear that he wasn't coming on to her, and she had a feeling he didn't have to overcompensate for anything.

Not that she'd ever be in a position to verify that, of course.

Did Kate have any idea how hot and bothered she'd made him?

He doubted it.

He'd always known she was clueless when it came to the practical side of life, and apparently that included dealing with men. Which was why he'd pushed her to let him take her home. She was like an angelfish swimming in shark-infested waters, and he couldn't count on the next guy who hit on her being like Arthur . . . or him.

Not that he was usually so noble. But Kate had had a lousy day, thanks in part to him, and she'd been drinking. That was the only reason he felt so protective of her.

It was guilt, plain and simple. Guilt and basic human decency, not to take advantage of a vulnerable woman.

He had a sudden, visceral memory of Kate's body against his. Sweet Christ. If it weren't for guilt and decency, he wouldn't even wait to get her home tonight. He'd drag her into a dark corner right here in the club, slide his hands under that tight little skirt, and—

A loud honk brought him out of his heated fantasy.

He'd almost walked into the street. Now he took a step back and looked around, spotting Stephen's Harley a few doors down.

By the time Kate came out of the club, he was waiting for her at the curb. Her eyes lit up when she saw the beautiful machine, and he couldn't help smiling at her enthusiasm.

The air had turned cool for a May evening. When Kate came up beside him, he pulled off his leather jacket and laid it across her shoulders.

"Thanks," she said, looking surprised and grateful as she put her arms through the sleeves. Then he handed her a helmet.

"This is my first time on a motorcycle," she confessed as she put it on. "I've always wanted to ride one."

"Of course you have. All right-minded people want to ride a motorcycle."

She started to climb on, and then hesitated. "I'm wearing a miniskirt," she said. "Doesn't this have the potential to be a little indecent?"

He shrugged. "I wouldn't worry about it. I'll be facing front, so I won't see anything—and that jacket's long enough to hide you from the rest of the world."

She thought about it for a moment and then nodded, swinging a leg over the passenger seat and settling in behind him, putting her hands lightly on his shoulders.

"You'll probably want to hang on a little tighter than that," he said.

31

He wasn't really concerned that she'd fall off—he wasn't planning to go that fast. But with a woman like Kate on his bike, he'd be a fool not to get her as close as possible.

He reached back to move her hands from his shoulders to his waist. Then he revved the engine, smiling to himself when her grip tightened instinctively.

"Where to, ma'am?"

"Seventy-Seventh between Columbus and Central Park West."

His eyebrows went up a trifle. That was a pretty swanky address. She lived on the Upper West Side near the Museum of Natural History, across the park from his even swankier address on the Upper East Side.

"Okay, here we go. All set back there?"

"Yes."

A lot of years had passed since he'd been on a bike, but it wasn't something he'd ever forget. As he pulled out into traffic, he found himself smiling—partly from the pleasure of being on a Harley again, and partly from the sensation of Kate's body molded to his, her breasts pressed against his back and her arms around his waist.

It took him twenty minutes to get uptown, which wasn't too bad for a Friday night. He didn't hurry, either. It was a beautiful night, and he wasn't in a rush for the ride to end.

Or to say goodbye to Kate.

As he turned down Seventy-Seventh, he remembered the scornful look she'd given him earlier in the day. It seemed almost surreal that he was taking her home on a Harley just ten hours later, the insides of her thighs pressed to the outsides of his.

It had been one hell of a night.

He pulled up in front of her building and turned off the engine. "Home sweet home," he said in the sudden quiet.

Kate didn't move. "That was so cool," she said almost wistfully. "I don't want it to be over."

Wondering briefly if he was making a mistake, he said, "It doesn't have to be over. I could take you on a longer ride if you want."

A moment of silence. Then: "That's a nice offer, but I guess I'll head inside. Thanks, though. And thanks for the ride. I loved it."

At least one of them knew when to put the brakes on.

"I'm glad."

The doorman was coming towards them, and Ian pulled off his helmet and hung it on a handlebar. "Is it okay if I park here for a few minutes?" he asked the man. "I'm going to walk Ms. Meredith to her door."

The doorman stared. "Ms. Meredith? I didn't recognize you. Of course, sir—you'll be fine there for half an hour."

"I won't be that long," Ian said easily. He slid off the bike and held out a hand to Kate.

She pulled off her own helmet and hung it on the other handlebar. That glorious copper hair of hers tumbled free, bouncing on her shoulders like living silk.

Why hadn't she ever worn it down at work?

Probably so men like him wouldn't adjust the front of their pants every time they looked at her.

Her face was flushed and she looked happy. She really had enjoyed the ride. "Are you sure you want to go up with me? You don't have to. This is a safe building, and Andreas is right here," she added, smiling at the doorman.

"Absolutely," he said firmly. "What kind of gentleman would I be if I just dropped you off at the curb?"

She shrugged. "All right, then."

Andreas held the door for them, and they stepped inside the elegant foyer.

"This is a nice building," he commented as they waited for the elevator. "And it's a great neighborhood."

He couldn't help wondering what the rent was like. What kind of savings did she have? Could she afford to go on living here after she'd lost her job?

He knew it was none of his business, but once they were inside the elevator he heard himself ask, "Are you going to be okay financially? While you're in, uh, transition?"

He hoped she was too tipsy to notice how inappropriate the question was.

She looked at him with one eyebrow up. "How sweet of you to ask, Mr. Hart. Especially since you're responsible for my 'transition.'"

Okay, she wasn't too tipsy. But he had to know. "I just wondered if you had a backup plan. For living expenses."

"My backup plan is the fact that I own my apartment. My grandparents left it to me. So I'm not going to be out on the streets, if that's what's worrying you," she added drily.

He was relieved to hear it, but at the same time, the knowledge that she came from money reinforced his old feeling about Kate—that she'd never had to struggle for anything. It was easy for someone born rich to be idealistic and creative and oblivious, and to turn up her nose at practical realities like ratings and market share and stockholders' meetings.

They arrived at the tenth floor, and the elevator opened. Kate crossed the hallway to apartment 10B and stopped in front of the door, pulling off his jacket and handing it to him.

"Thanks again for the ride—and for offering to be my date to the wedding from hell." She spoke a little coolly, and Ian wasn't sure if he was relieved or disappointed that he'd managed to dissipate any lingering electricity between them.

"No problem."

She fished her key out of her purse, unlocked the door, and then paused with her hand on the knob. "Do you want to come in?" she asked, without noticeable enthusiasm. "I've got wine if you want a drink."

He shook his head. "That's all right. I should be getting home."

"Okay." She was looking at him now with a little frown between her brows, and he wondered what she was thinking.

"So what's the deal with the tattoos?" she asked suddenly. "Do I get to hear that story?"

"Maybe someday," he said, deflecting the question. He didn't usually talk about his past, and the longer he stood here, gazing into Kate's blue eyes and breathing in her subtle fragrance, the harder it was to remember all the good reasons not to kiss her.

He cleared his throat and took a deliberate step back. "I'll keep the weekend of the twelfth open. Good night, Kate."

"Good night, Ian."

She opened the door, gave him a quick smile, and disappeared inside.

That was the first time she'd ever called him by his first name.

When he realized he was still staring at her door a minute later, he turned and headed for the elevator.

There was no reason to look forward to an event Kate had described as "the wedding from hell." But as he gunned Stephen's Harley and drove away, that was exactly what he was doing.

Chapter Three

When Kate woke up the next morning, she opened her eyes to find Gallifrey staring at her from a distance of three inches. He was sitting on her chest like a library lion, gazing down with sphinxlike majesty.

"Go away," she told him, even as she reached up to scratch between his ears. His low, rusty purr vibrated through her.

She had a headache, and her mouth tasted like the bottom of a birdcage. What the hell had she—

Oh, God.

Memory came flooding back in a sickening wave. Her show . . . Chris . . . the club last night and three shots of whiskey.

Three shots of whiskey . . . and Ian Hart.

Oh, *God*.

She replayed the evening's events in her head, trying to remember everything that had happened with Ian.

Okay, she hadn't kissed him. That was good.

On the other hand, she'd wrapped herself around him on the dance floor and on the motorcycle.

The motorcycle . . .

Kate closed her eyes as she remembered that ride. It really was like having power between your legs. Maybe that's what made it so sexy—as sexy as their dance had been. Her body pressed against

Ian's, her arms around that rock-hard abdomen . . . feeling the bunch and release of his muscles as he wove through traffic . . .

Hoo, boy.

And he'd offered to be her date to Jessica's wedding.

Gallifrey, who had apparently decided the time for Zen-like meditation was over, interrupted her thoughts. He kneaded her chest through the cotton sheet, the prick of his claws causing her to say, "Ow, ow, ow," before she sat up in bed and ran her hands through her hair.

Since sitting up was her usual prelude to getting out of bed and feeding him, Gallifrey jumped to the floor and headed for the kitchen.

As soon as he was gone, Kate collapsed back on her pillow. She felt like crap, though she would've felt a lot worse if she'd stayed at the club last night and continued drinking shots.

Ian had kept her from doing that. And he'd kept her from going home with a stranger, too.

He'd looked out for her. And he hadn't been too heavy-handed about it, all things considered.

In fact, he'd been pretty nice.

Well, why not? He owed her, didn't he? They'd both agreed on that.

She turned her head and looked at the clock. Was it really almost noon? She hadn't slept this late in years.

"*Mrrowr!*"

That was Gallifrey, sitting in the bedroom doorway with a disgusted look on his face.

"I'm coming, I'm coming. Give me a minute."

Coffee and a shower would make her feel more human, and the cat wouldn't leave her alone until he got his breakfast. She might as well get up.

A few minutes later, Gallifrey was eating and Kate was pouring milk into her coffee. The thought of food was not appealing, so she took her mug into the living room, curled up in the armchair by the window, and took her first sustaining sip of caffeine.

The day ahead of her was depressingly blank. If she didn't find some way to keep busy, she'd definitely start feeling sorry for herself.

The first item on her agenda would have to be uninviting Ian to Jessica's wedding. That had been an arrangement made in the heat of rejection and under the influence of alcohol.

She'd thank him for the offer—as galling as it was to have to thank the man who'd cancelled her show for anything—but explain that she'd be just fine going to the wedding alone. She was a strong, self-confident woman, and she didn't need a crutch to face her ex-fiancé.

Although the thought of sweeping into the reception hall with Ian Hart on her arm was very, very tempting.

In more ways than one.

And that was the other reason she needed to cancel this fake date. The last thing she needed while navigating the waters of unemployment and a broken engagement was the confusing distraction of lustful feelings for a man she'd always despised.

So it was decided. She'd take a shower, get dressed, and jot down a few bullet points about what she'd say. Once she was well prepared, she'd sit down at her desk and make the call.

Her phone rang.

She was so lost in thought she jumped, spilling coffee down the front of her pajamas. The phone was on the table next to the armchair, and she grabbed for it as she pulled off her stained pajama top, using it to sop up the coffee that had spilled on the floor.

"Hello?"

"Is this Kate Meredith?"

It was Ian.

An electric feeling went through her. Unable to speak, she froze with the phone in her hand.

This was the exact opposite of the circumstances in which she'd wanted this conversation to take place. She'd planned to be distant, polite, well prepared, and fully clothed. Instead, she was kneeling in a puddle of coffee with her hair sticking up in all directions . . . and she was topless.

Of course, since this was a phone call, there was no reason Ian had to know any of that. She could still *sound* fully clothed, right? She cleared her throat. "Yes, this is Kate."

"Hi, Kate. It's Ian Hart."

No kidding. "Hi, Ian."

There was a moment of silence, and Kate was about to say something to fill it, when she stopped herself. He was the one who'd called her, after all. It was up to him to tell her what he wanted.

Oh, God—she knew what he wanted. He was going to cancel on Jessica's wedding.

Well, that was good. Right? It was the same thing she wanted.

Except she'd been planning to ditch him, instead of the other way around.

"You're probably wondering why I called. This is a little embarrassing, but—"

"It's fine," she interrupted. "I know what you're going to say."

"You do?" He sounded bewildered, and Kate wondered suddenly if she might be wrong.

"I . . . that is . . . why don't you tell me?" she said after a moment, wishing like hell she had clothes on. The sound of Ian's sexy baritone voice affected her like a caress, causing her bare nipples to pucker and tighten.

She went over to the couch and grabbed the quilt she kept there, wrapping it around her torso before sitting down. That was a little better.

"Okay. Here's the thing." He hesitated, and Kate bit her lip. He *was* going to cancel on her.

"I was at the club last night for a bachelor party. My friend's wedding is tonight, and my babysitter just cancelled on me."

Babysitter? Ian had *kids*?

No—that couldn't be. There was no way the female employees

at the network, who had assembled quite a dossier on him, would have missed that piece of personal info.

"I didn't realize you had children," she said cautiously.

"I don't. It's my nephew. He's been living with me since his mother died."

His mother. Was that Ian's sister?

"It's an adults-only reception, and even though I'm sure my friend would understand if I had to bring Jacob, it would be awkward. And since he's eleven, I'm sure the last thing he wants to do is go to a wedding—especially when he'd be the only kid there."

Was he looking for recommendations for professional babysitters? The best ones wouldn't be available on short notice, but—

"I've tried a few services, but they're booked up. And anyway, I'd be more comfortable with someone I know." He paused. "Unfortunately, anyone I know well enough to ask for a favor like this is going to Mick's wedding, too."

The reason for Ian's call finally dawned on her.

He needed a babysitter.

A swirl of emotions went through her. Relief that he wasn't blowing her off for Jessica's wedding, even though she had every intention of blowing him off. Annoyance that he thought he knew *her* well enough to ask a favor like this. And underneath all that, an unexpected feeling of disappointment. A part of her had wondered if maybe, just maybe, he was calling to ask her out on a real date.

Which was crazy, of course. He'd made it clear last night that he had no romantic intentions towards her, and even if she weren't still reeling from a breakup, Ian Hart was the last man on earth she'd want to go out with.

"So," he continued, "I was wondering if you might be willing to do it. I'd send a car to pick you up and take you home again, and of course I'd pay you whatever you think is fair."

He was offering to *pay* her? Why, that—

"I wouldn't ask if I wasn't desperate," he went on. "Jacob's had a rough time since his mom died, and he's always been kind of an introvert. I'd hate to drag him to this wedding, even if other kids were going to be there."

Now she'd feel guilty for saying no. She could lie and say she was busy, but—

"I can do it," she heard herself say.

"Really? That's great." The relief in his voice was palpable. "Do you want me to pay you an hourly rate or a fixed sum for the night?"

It was then that Kate realized one of the reasons she'd said yes to this.

"I don't want you to pay me at all. I'll watch your nephew because I'm a nice person. I remember you said once that there's no such thing as a nice person—that when someone does you a favor, there's always an agenda involved. The only thing I want in exchange for helping you out is an acknowledgment that you were wrong about that."

"Oh, for God's sake," Ian said, sounding disgusted.

Kate found herself smiling. "It's a pretty small price to pay for free babysitting."

A short silence. "What exactly do you want me to say?"

"Just that people can do nice things without having an agenda. I'm sure you can manage to utter the words without actually choking on them."

"But you *do* have an agenda. You want me to say that there's true kindness in the world, or whatever. That's an agenda."

"All right, then. Good luck finding another—"

"Fine, I'll say it. There may, on rare occasions, be people who do nice things just for the sake of being nice. Is that good enough?"

She was still smiling. "Yep, that'll do. What time do you need me tonight?"

"The babysitter was supposed to come at five o'clock, but if that's too early I could—"

"Five o'clock is fine."

"I won't be home until after midnight."

"That's fine, too. You're sending me home in a car, right?"

"Right." He paused. "So . . . I'll send my driver to pick you up at five. He'll call when he's downstairs."

"Sounds good."

Another pause. "Okay, then," he said after a moment. "I guess I'll see you later today. And . . . thanks, Kate."

"You're welcome."

It occurred to her after she hung up that she still had to cancel their date to Jessica's wedding. But when she went into the bathroom to shower, she saw Chris's toothbrush on the sink and felt a sudden spasm in her throat.

She and Chris had met a year earlier at Jessica's engagement party. He was a biology professor and, like her, not much of a party person. They'd bonded in a quiet corner to which they'd both retreated to get away from the crowd. Their friendship had begun that night, and a few months later they'd started dating.

The transition had been smooth and effortless. They got along as a couple as well as they did as friends—they rarely argued, and there was no drama or angst between them. When Chris had proposed two months ago, it had seemed like the natural culmination of their relationship. Add in the fact that Kate was twenty-nine—right on the cusp between not-a-kid-anymore and holy-biological-clock, Batman—and their engagement had felt almost inevitable.

A part of her had wondered if she ought to be more excited about the whole thing, but she'd long ago come to the conclusion that there would always be a gap between the romances she read and wrote about and the ones she experienced in real life. And Chris was a kind, intelligent, gentle man, and she loved and trusted him.

At least, she had until he'd fallen in love with someone else.

How could she have been so blindsided by someone she thought she knew? Had there been signs all along—signs she'd missed? Their relationship might not have lit the world on fire, but up until yesterday she'd thought it was solid. She'd thought they wanted the same things and were looking forward to building a life together.

But Chris, it turned out, had been looking for something else. Some*one* else. Someone who made him feel whatever it was Anastasia made him feel.

Someone who wasn't her.

She picked up his toothbrush and squeezed it in her hand.

They'd spent more nights at his place than at hers, but he did have some clothes in the closet and some toiletries here in the bathroom. The clothes she'd give back to him, but a spare toothbrush she could—and did—throw out.

Once she'd dropped it in the wastebasket, she scoured the bathroom for other remnants of him. She found an old bottle of aftershave, a razor, a stick of deodorant, and an empty prescription bottle. They followed the toothbrush into the trash.

She stared down at the pitiful detritus of her relationship. When she felt a tickle in her nose and the sting of tears behind her eyes, she grabbed the basket, marched out of the apartment, and emptied it into the garbage chute.

Back inside, she told herself there was no need to uninvite Ian to Jessica's wedding just yet. What if she decided she did need a crutch to face her ex? If she'd already cancelled on Ian, she'd be too embarrassed to reinvite him.

Maybe she should give it a few days and see how she felt.

After her shower, she made some toast and poured another cup of coffee. She had only a few hours before she was due at Ian's, so she decided to stay home and look through her project folder—the file of story ideas she hoped to get to someday.

She'd published short stories and graphic novels before she'd gotten her first job as a television writer. She'd worked on a few different shows in the years since then, but *Life with Max* had been her baby. She'd created it, and she'd written and directed most of the episodes herself with the help of a wonderful production team.

As much as she'd enjoyed doing the show, it had been pretty demanding. She'd sometimes wished she had a little more free time to explore other projects.

Well, now she did. Not by choice, of course, but still.

She should have seen the writing on the wall. Her ratings had been slipping this season, especially after the network had changed her time slot. But even though she should know better by now, she'd stupidly assumed that the Emmy they'd won the previous year and the glowing reviews the show always received would carry more weight with the network execs.

Just how naive was she, anyway? She hadn't seen the cancellation coming any more than she'd predicted Chris's infidelity. Because she was a person who always tried to stick with things, she'd expected the network and her fiancé to stick with her.

But, damn it, she wouldn't let this change her. She'd learn from the experience and move on, but she wouldn't give up her values and ideals. She just needed to find a better home for them, that was all.

And she needed to learn how to protect herself a little better.

This weekend she'd think about what she wanted to work on next, and Monday she'd start making calls to set up pitches. She wouldn't feel sorry for herself, and she wouldn't let the grass grow under her feet. She'd get right out there and make something happen.

Unfortunately, she didn't find the inspiration she was looking for. None of her old project ideas seemed to get her creative juices flowing.

Maybe she needed a new project. Something fresh and exciting. And maybe she should get away from TV for a while. She could pitch a graphic novel or a children's adventure story to a publisher, or—

The phone rang, and she picked it up absently.

"Ms. Meredith? There's a car here for you."

Damn. Was it five o'clock already?

"I'll be right down."

She'd planned to put on a little makeup and choose the perfect outfit—something flattering while also appropriate for babysitting. There'd been masculine approval in Ian's eyes the night before, and she didn't want to look so crappy today that he would decide her appearance in the club had been just an aberration. That wouldn't be good for her ego.

But now she didn't have any time.

Oh, well—maybe the best way to look like she wasn't trying too hard was not to try too hard. She kept on her jeans and vintage X-Men tee shirt, pulled her hair back in a ponytail, and headed out.

∼

Ian knocked on his nephew's door and waited for the quiet "come in" before he turned the knob.

"Hey," he said. "It's almost five o'clock. Kate will be here soon."

Jacob looked up from his computer and nodded. "Okay."

Ian waited a moment to see if he'd say anything else, but he didn't. He just blinked behind his wire-rimmed glasses and smiled politely.

"Okay," Ian echoed after a short silence, retreating back into the hall and closing the door behind him.

His sister Tina, Jacob's mother, had died in a car accident eleven months earlier. Ian still couldn't think of it without a spasm of pain.

Jacob's father, Joe, had been killed in Afghanistan before Jacob was born. Ian and Tina had never known their father and their mother had passed away, so except for Joe's parents, Ian was the only family Jacob had left.

In her will, Tina had named Ian her son's legal guardian. He had been humbled by his sister's trust in him and was determined to do right by his nephew.

It was a resolution easier made than kept.

His nephew had always been a quiet boy, and the two of them had never really connected. But since Jacob had come here to live, he'd been more than quiet. He'd been silent and withdrawn.

For the first few months, Ian had respected Jacob's obvious desire to spend his free time alone, figuring that was his way of dealing with his grief. Ian made it clear he was ready to listen if Jacob wanted to talk, but beyond that, he didn't push his nephew to interact with him.

But when the school year began, Ian started to worry that Jacob's behavior was more than a normal response to the loss of a parent. If his nephew had mouthed off or acted out, Ian would have known better how to deal with him. But he'd never been around a kid who was so . . . remote.

In the fall, Ian pushed him to try out for his school's soccer team—or any sports team. Jacob had refused, politely but firmly. Ian took him to games—baseball, football, basketball—but Jacob always brought a book along. When Ian tried to talk him into going to the park to toss a Frisbee or a football around, Jacob always turned him down.

As Ian grew more worried, he wondered if he should take his nephew to see a therapist. Not only to help him deal with his mother's death, but in case he had Asperger syndrome or something on that spectrum.

Whatever was going on with Jacob, Ian felt out of his depth. They'd been living together for almost a year and nothing had changed. Jacob's grades were good, and his teachers spoke highly of him, but they also noticed that he kept to himself and seemed to have little interest in making friends.

The intercom buzzed. "Mr. Hart? Kate Meredith is on her way up."

"Thanks, Harvey."

What he'd told Kate was true: he hadn't had many options for Jacob tonight. The agencies he'd called were booked up, the two young people in the building he trusted to babysit were busy, and his closest friends would be at the wedding.

But he hadn't called Kate only as a last resort. Other factors—ones he wasn't all that eager to admit to—had been part of his decision.

There was the fact that if Kate were over here, she wouldn't be at a nightclub, hooking up with a stranger. And if Kate were over here, he'd get to see her again.

He told himself that desperation was the main reason he'd called her and that anything else was a minor factor at best. Then he remembered their conversation and found himself smiling.

Somehow, he wasn't surprised at the price Kate had demanded for helping him out—not money, but a concession that people could be unselfish. That was the naive, idealistic Kate he knew.

He was looking forward to seeing her again and putting her back in the box he'd always kept her in: charming but infuriating, and definitely not someone he was interested in sexually.

Last night had been unsettling for both of them. It would be good to get back on more familiar footing, but with a little more civility and mutual respect between them.

There was a knock on the door, and he went to open it.

He'd planned to give Kate an easy, friendly greeting—something that would make it clear that the previous night's interaction had been an anomaly, the consequence of alcohol and her bad day.

But when he opened the door and saw her standing there, the words died on his lips.

She didn't look anything like the sexy vixen of the night before, but it didn't matter. His body reacted the same way—hardening and tightening, his heartbeat quickening.

She was wearing a pair of old, worn jeans that showcased her long legs, and a faded tee shirt she filled out impressively. She wore no makeup and her eyes looked a little tired, but they were still beautiful—dark blue and fringed with thick lashes.

As for those soft, full lips . . .

He cleared his throat. "Hi, Kate. Thanks again for doing this."

"No problem. Do you need help with that?"

She was looking below his chin, and he realized she meant his bow tie, which hung loose around his neck.

"Uh . . . sure. Okay."

It took her only about ten seconds, which was fairly impressive. He concentrated on keeping his eyes away from her cleavage.

She stepped back with satisfaction. "What do you think?" she asked, nodding towards the mirror that hung next to the coat rack.

He stepped in front of it, putting himself shoulder to shoulder with Kate. He knew he was supposed to be looking at the tie, but for a moment all he could see was the two of them.

When she wasn't in heels, the top of her head was about level with his chin.

Perfect kissing distance.

She was smiling at him in the mirror, and he smiled back. "It looks great," he said, even though he hadn't so much as glanced at the tie. When he did, though, he found it was true.

"Do you moonlight as a valet?" he asked, as he gestured for her to precede him into the living room.

"I have three brothers," she explained, looking around the big room. He'd hired someone to decorate when he'd first moved in, and it had turned out okay, if a little too beige for his taste.

He wondered suddenly what Kate thought of it. He had a feeling she wasn't big on beige.

"Three brothers," he repeated. "Older or younger?"

"One older, two younger," she said, turning away from the window.

"So, do you want to fill me in on the essentials? Emergency numbers, food preferences, bedtime?"

Jacob. Right. The reason she was here.

He took her into the kitchen and showed her around, pointing out the emergency numbers and other information on the refrigerator door.

"He's a pretty quiet kid," he said, using the phrases he always did when talking to a new babysitter. "He won't give you any trouble, and he'll probably spend most of the night in his room. Bedtime is nine o'clock, and he doesn't have any food allergies. There's frozen stuff in the freezer to microwave for dinner."

Kate nodded. "Sounds good. Can you introduce me?"

"Sure."

A minute later, he was knocking on his nephew's door again.

"Come in," came the subdued reply, and Ian led the way into the room.

"Jacob, this is my friend Kate Meredith." He'd hesitated an instant before using the word *friend*, but figured it was better than *former coworker*.

"Hi, Jacob," Kate said with a smile. "How's it going?"

"Fine," Jacob said politely, turning in his desk chair to face her. Unexpectedly, his eyes lit up. "Hey, the X-Men!"

His eyes were on Kate's chest, and for one horrified instant Ian thought he was looking at her breasts. Then he realized it was the tee shirt that had caught Jacob's eye.

Kate nodded. "Can you name the mutants?"

"Of course. Rogue, Wolverine, and Gambit."

Kate's eyebrows went up. "Impressive. Everyone knows Wolverine, and it's fifty-fifty with Rogue, but Gambit's usually a stumper."

Jacob was grinning, something Ian didn't see too often. "I named my cat Remeow LeBeau."

Kate laughed out loud while Ian wondered what was so funny.

"I don't get it," he said after a moment.

It was Kate who explained. "Gambit's one of the X-Men. His real name is Remy LeBeau. Get it? Remy, Remeow? It's genius."

Still feeling a little out of it, Ian nodded. "Very clever."

"So where is Mr. LeBeau?" Kate asked. "Can I meet him?"

Jacob's face clouded over. "This building doesn't allow pets. When I moved here, I had to give him to my neighbors back home in White Plains. They send me pictures and stuff, though. Do you want to see one?"

"Sure."

Ian frowned. One of the few times Jacob had shown any emotion in front of him was when he'd found out he couldn't bring his cat to the city. He'd actually cried about it, and Ian had done his best to be comforting, although he probably wasn't as sympathetic as someone who actually liked cats would have been.

He'd thought he hid his aversion pretty well, but maybe not. Jacob had never suggested showing him a picture of his pet.

Determined to seem interested now, he came up beside Kate to look at Jacob's computer screen, which showed a big orange cat lounging on the back of a sofa.

"Oh, he's beautiful," Kate said. "I love orange cats. Mine's a tuxedo."

"Tuxedo cats are awesome. What's his name?"

"Gallifrey." Kate said the name with a note of challenge in her voice, as if to say, *Let's see if you can figure that one out.*

Ian was glad the challenge wasn't directed his way. The name Gallifrey meant nothing to him—but then, neither had Remeow LeBeau. These two were obviously engaging in some kind of geek-speak, and he didn't have a decoder ring.

"Doctor Who's home planet!" Jacob exclaimed. "That's *awesome.*"

His nephew watched British television? Who knew?

Ian glanced at his watch. "I guess I should be going," he said, even though he almost wished he could stay. It was rare to see Jacob this talkative.

Kate nodded. "I'll walk you out." She smiled at Jacob. "When I come back, we can talk about dinner, okay? Maybe you can help me pick something out."

"Sure."

As they walked through the living room, Ian said, "I have to tell you, Kate—I've never seen Jacob take to anyone that quickly. The truth is, I've been worried about him. I'm afraid he might have Asperger syndrome or something like that."

Kate looked at him in surprise. "Asperger's? I don't think so. He's probably just having a tough time dealing with his mother's death, like you said before. That's natural."

Ian nodded. "I know. I've tried to help, but I haven't made a lot of progress." He paused at the door. "Anyway, it's obvious I'm leaving him in good hands. Call me if you have any questions or if you need anything."

"I will. Have a good time at the wedding, Ian."

His eyes held hers for a moment. "Thanks."

On his way downstairs, he looked at his bow tie in the mirrored wall of the elevator. Seeing it made him remember Kate standing close to him, her hands working quickly and skillfully at his neck.

He didn't usually like women fussing over him, which was probably one of the many reasons his relationships never lasted very long. But he hadn't minded when Kate did it.

It had seemed almost natural.

He checked his watch as the elevator doors opened. He was running a few minutes late, but he should still be at the church in plenty of time.

Mick Kalen was one of his oldest friends, and he'd been looking forward to this wedding for months. But as he stepped out of his apartment building and into the cool May evening, he wasn't thinking about his destination.

He was thinking about the two people he'd left behind.

∿

All through the wedding and the reception, Ian's thoughts kept returning to Kate. A little after eleven o'clock, he was dancing with the bride's sister, a bubbly, cheerful woman named Shelly. Their moves on the dance floor couldn't have been more different from his dance with Kate last night.

Just thinking about it sent a wave of lust through his body.

He'd forgotten how sexy it could be just to dance with a woman. He and Kate had fit together so well . . . and because she'd been a little tipsy and a little unsteady in her high heels, she'd let him hold her close.

He could still feel her breasts against his chest and the satin softness of the bare skin at her waist. He could still smell her fragrance—not a heavy perfume, but a faint suggestion of jasmine. He remembered her *mmmmmmm* of pleasure, and the way she'd stiffened afterward when she'd realized she'd made the sound out loud.

But when his hands had tightened on her, she hadn't pulled away. She had even seemed to soften a little, and the yielding quality in the way she'd moved against him had made his body harden in response.

"Ian? Are you all right?"

He opened his eyes to see Shelly looking at him with a concerned expression on her face.

"I'm fine," he said, realizing that he'd stopped dancing. "I just remembered I have to . . . call the babysitter."

"Oh my goodness, I know what that's like. You should go take care of that right away."

"I probably should," he said, since the song was ending. "Thanks for the dance," he added with a smile.

A few minutes later he was in the hotel lobby, pacing back and forth with his cell phone in his hand. If he called, Kate would tell him everything was fine and that he shouldn't hurry back. On the other hand, if he left now, he'd be home in half an hour. It wasn't midnight yet—it wouldn't be too late to offer Kate a drink before she went home.

They'd already done the big send-off for the bride and groom, so there was no reason he couldn't leave the reception now.

Forty minutes later, he was turning his key in his lock.

The apartment was silent, so he moved quietly down the hall and into the living room. Other than the ambient city light that came in through the windows, the room was dark.

It took him a moment to spot Kate asleep on the couch. He walked over and stood looking down at her.

She was curled up on her side with her cheek pillowed on her hand, her chest rising and falling gently. Her lips were slightly parted. Her feet were bare, and he was surprised to see that her toenails were painted red.

He never would have guessed that Kate Meredith used red toenail polish.

He started to feel uncomfortable. Watching her sleep seemed too intimate, like an invasion of privacy.

"Hey there," he said softly.

She didn't stir, and he put a hand on her shoulder. "Wake up, Sleeping Beauty."

Her eyes opened. She looked confused for a moment; then she smiled at him and stretched.

"Hey," she said, her voice sounding sleepy. "How was the wedding?"

Kate's soft voice in the dark room deepened the illusion of intimacy. He had a crazy urge to kiss her hello, as if they'd been married for years.

He took a step back instead.

"It was good. How was Jacob?"

"He was great."

She sat up and yawned, covering her mouth with one hand. Her hair had come loose from its ponytail, and it looked silky and tousled and sexy as hell.

He had to clench his hands into fists to keep from touching it.

"He doesn't have Asperger's," Kate went on. "You've just been using the wrong approach with him."

He was so distracted by his physical response to her that it took a moment to register what she'd said.

He frowned. "What do you mean, the 'wrong approach'?"

"You've been pushing him to do all this sports stuff, and he hates sports. He's afraid you don't like him because he's not athletic. You need to back off all that and talk to him about things he's actually interested in."

As her words sank in, his hackles rose. "How would he know if he hates sports? He won't even try them."

Kate shook her head. "Of course he's tried them. There's not an eleven-year-old boy in America who hasn't been forced to try sports at some point. His mom put him in Little League and peewee soccer when he was five, and he stuck with it for two years. But he hated it so much that she finally let him quit."

Defensiveness made his voice sharp. "Exercise is important. Childhood obesity is a huge problem in this country. I want Jacob to be fit and healthy."

"Well, sure. But team sports aren't the only way to get exercise. Jacob really loves to swim, for example. And swimming is one of the best forms of exercise there is. Problem solved."

"Just like that, huh?"

Kate stared at him. He knew he sounded sarcastic, but he didn't apologize.

"It's not only about exercise," he said. "Team sports teach you about sportsmanship and discipline. And they're a way to make friends."

"There are other ways to accomplish those goals. Jacob likes chess. He could join a chess club, and—"

"A *chess* club? Jesus. Maybe he should join the math team and the A/V club, too."

Kate's eyebrows drew together. "What's that supposed to mean?"

"I don't want Jacob to be a social outcast. I don't want him to get bullied or teased. Is there something wrong with that?"

He heard the edge in his voice, but he didn't try to soften it. Who the hell did Kate think she was? She'd waltzed in here and spent a few hours with Jacob, and now she thought she knew what was best for him?

Ian had gone through a lot of different phases as a kid. He'd been the boy who didn't fit in and the boy who did. And when he was older, he'd been a teenager who got into all kinds of trouble.

It didn't seem likely that Jacob would go down that third path, and Ian would do everything in his power to make sure he didn't. But between the first two choices, Ian knew which one would be easier on his nephew.

Kate, on the other hand, had grown up soft. She didn't have a clue what it was like to be a boy who didn't play sports. A boy who was perceived as weak.

She was still frowning at him. "Letting Jacob do the things he enjoys doesn't automatically mean he'll be bullied. What you're doing is giving him the message that there's something wrong with who he actually is. You're trying to make him into someone he's not."

"I'm just trying to teach him how to survive. Of course, I'm not surprised you don't understand that. You've never had to survive, have you? You were born with a silver spoon in your mouth, and I'm sure you've been Mommy and Daddy's spoiled princess your whole life. You never had to struggle to put a roof over your head or food on the table. But life's a little harsher for the rest of us, Kate. Most people have to figure out how to adapt to their surroundings. They don't expect everyone else to adapt to them."

Kate sprang to her feet. "Are you saying *I* expect that? That's ridiculous. And points for the hypocrisy, by the way. I love that you're accusing *me* of being spoiled while you're standing in your soulless palace of luxury—and after I spent the night babysitting for you."

She folded her arms. "I'm not a spoiled brat, in spite of your charming description of me. Is that why you cancelled my show, Hart? Because you think I'm some kind of diva? I know you never liked me, but—"

"Of course you would say that. You refuse to pay attention to ratings and financials, and then you accuse me of cancelling your show for personal reasons." He took a breath. "First of all, it wasn't only my decision. Everyone in upper management has to sign off on schedule changes. Your show got cancelled because it was losing market share and ad revenue, as you would know if you paid any attention in weekly meetings. This isn't public television and we're not running a charity. We have to answer to our shareholders and our—"

"You also have to answer to your viewers. *Life with Max* received more fan mail than any other children's program on the network."

"I'm not saying the fans aren't loyal. You did two great seasons, and in this age of DVDs and video streaming, those shows will always be available to anyone who wants to find them. But we can no longer justify investing in new episodes. The decision wasn't personal, Kate. There's no need to get defensive or—"

"You're accusing *me* of being defensive? You're the one who jumped down my throat when I talked to you about your nephew."

He felt another flare of anger. "You've got no right to talk to me about Jacob. You don't know anything about him or his situation or—"

"I know he's unhappy. And I know you're a big part of that."

For just an instant, the fear that Kate might be right washed over him in a sickening wave. Then anger drowned out his insecurity. "I love Jacob. I want what's best for him. And considering that I'm a successful executive and you're an unemployed writer who couldn't hang onto her fiancé, I think I know which of our opinions I have more confidence in."

As soon as the words were out of his mouth, he wished he could unsay them. Kate's head jerked back as though he'd slapped her across the face, and in the instant before she shuttered all expression, he saw the hurt in her eyes.

Maybe it wasn't too late to fix it. "I'm sorry, Kate. I shouldn't have—"

"Get out of my way, Hart."

She pushed past him and went towards the foyer, where she put on her shoes and grabbed her purse.

He followed her to his front door, feeling like the biggest asshole on the planet. "Please let me apologize."

She turned with her hand on the knob, her expression as cold and contemptuous as it had ever been. "I feel sorry for your nephew—he deserves better than you. He's the one you should apologize to."

"Kate—"

"Save it. And in case there was any doubt, I won't need your help to face my ex at the wedding from hell. I'd rather have one jerk to deal with than two."

And then she was gone.

Chapter Four

Kate went to sleep pissed off and woke up pissed off. When she thought about her own stupidity—putting herself in a position that allowed Ian Hart to do more damage to her ego—she wasn't sure which of them she was more angry with.

She shouldn't feel hurt by what he'd said. He shouldn't have the power to hurt her at all. If she hadn't fallen for his chivalrous act at the club, last night's scene wouldn't have happened.

That's what she got for letting her guard down . . . and for letting a man rescue her. A kick in the balls, metaphorically speaking.

It took two cups of coffee with Gallifrey purring on her lap before she started to feel better.

Then her cell phone rang.

When she saw it was Chris, she almost let it go to voice mail. But he was probably calling about his clothes, and the sooner she got the last remnants of him out of here, the better.

"Hi, Chris," she said.

"Hi."

A brilliant beginning.

There was a long pause. Finally she said impatiently, "Are you calling about your clothes? You can pick them up or I can send them to your apartment, whichever you'd—"

"That's not it."

Another silence. While she waited for him to break it, Kate tried to understand what she was feeling towards him.

Two nights ago, in front of the club, her heart had soared when she'd thought Chris was calling her. Now he actually *was* calling her, and she felt . . . what?

She wasn't sure. There was a knot of emotion in her chest she couldn't untangle—pain and sadness and bewilderment and anger.

Chris's betrayal had cut like a knife, the hurt made worse by the fact that she hadn't seen it coming. They'd been dating for eight months and engaged for two. They hadn't moved in together, but she spent two or three nights a week at his place and he spent one or two at hers, and they'd had all the ease and familiarity of an intimacy that was as much about friendship as it was about romantic love.

Romantic love . . .

Was that what she and Chris had had?

If romantic love was about being comfortable with another person, then yes.

If it was about heat and chemistry and passion, then no.

Wait. What?

Their sex life might have been a little tame, but she and Chris must have had *some* chemistry. Right?

And then, unbidden, the memory of two nights ago swept through her body, leaving tingles and goose bumps in its wake.

No, no, *no*.

She was not going to compare Chris with Ian. That was insane. Chris was the man she'd wanted to share her life with, have kids with, grow old with. Ian was the rude, arrogant, money-focused corporate bureaucrat who'd cancelled her show, roped her into babysitting for him, and then insulted her.

"Kate?"

She took a deep breath. "I'm still here."

"Could I . . . could we . . . Would it be all right if I came over? I think we should talk."

That was the phrase he'd used two days ago, right before he'd told her about Anastasia. But even though he couldn't break up with her twice, she didn't really want to see him right now.

"I don't think so, Chris. Maybe after some time has gone by we could—"

"Please, Kate. I have to talk to you. I know you don't owe me anything, but . . . please."

He was right about one thing: she didn't owe him. But maybe if she saw him again it would help her achieve some closure. "Well . . . I guess that would be all right."

"Good. Great. I'll be there in an hour."

She spent the hour curled up on the couch with a book, trying not to think about Chris or Ian. When her attention drifted, she added a few more panels to the comic strip in her head called *Why Cats Are Better Than Men*.

Andreas buzzed to let her know that Chris was on his way up, and Kate steeled herself for the meeting. When his knock came she opened the door.

Chris smiled at her nervously. His light blue eyes were anxious and his thick blond hair was mussed, as though he'd been running his hands through it. "Hi, Kate."

"Hi." She stood back to let him in, nodding politely.

How could you go from sharing a bed with someone to this stiff, awkward formality in less than forty-eight hours?

They sat down across from each other in the living room, she in an armchair and he on the couch. Chris crossed his legs, the way he did when he was nervous, and sat without speaking, his teeth sunk in his lower lip.

She was determined to make him speak first. He was the one who'd wanted to talk.

After what felt like five minutes but was probably more like thirty seconds, Chris finally said, "Thanks for letting me come by."

"Sure."

"I want . . ." He paused to clear his throat. "I want to apologize for the way I handled things on Friday."

He was sorry for the way he'd *handled* things? "It might be more to the point to apologize for cheating on me, but okay."

He flushed. "I didn't mean to cheat on you. I mean . . . I didn't realize what was happening with Anastasia until it was too late."

If she'd thought she could hear about his other woman without a pang, she'd been wrong.

"What the hell kind of name is Anastasia?" she heard herself snap. "Is she heir to the Romanovs, or what?"

He flinched. "Anastasia is . . . Anastasia is . . ." His hands fluttered in the air a moment before coming to rest on his knees. "Anastasia is gone."

She stared at him. "What do you mean, gone?"

"She left for Mexico this morning. Or maybe Brazil. I can't remember exactly what she said. She . . . she's very . . . spontaneous."

"Is she."

Chris took a deep breath. "I was a jerk to you on Friday. I know that. I just . . . I was starting to feel trapped in our relationship. Like I couldn't breathe. And then I met Anastasia, and she was so wild, so free . . ."

The implication being that she wasn't.

A sudden wave of depression went through her. Chris had said all this on Friday, and she didn't want to hear it again. Was this why he'd come over? To restate all the ways their relationship had been boring and predictable?

All the ways *she* was boring and predictable?

"But then, after she left this morning, I did some thinking. And I realized that I can't have it all. No one can. Maybe this whole . . . episode . . . was just my version of wedding jitters or a midlife crisis or something."

"A midlife crisis? You're thirty-two."

"Well, something else, then. To tell the truth, I'm not convinced that monogamy is a natural state for humans. Especially for men. I mean, think about it. Men are programmed to spread their seed as widely as possible. To propagate the species in a way that gives the greatest chance for survival."

Kate rubbed a hand over her eyes. Chris was a biology professor, and he voiced ideas like this occasionally. She'd always found his tendency to opine about human sexuality and natural selection sort of quirky and endearing, but she'd assumed his theories were just that: theories. It had never occurred to her that he might want to live his life according to them. To obey a biological imperative to "spread his seed as widely as possible."

"Look, Chris—"

"Let me finish. I'm just saying that modern man has to come to grips with the paradox of his body telling him one thing and his mind another. Right? So . . . I've come to grips with it."

For the life of her, she couldn't imagine where he was going with this.

"I don't—"

"I want *you*, Kate."

She blinked.

He was leaning forward now, his expression earnest. "I was a fool over Anastasia, but I learned something from the experience. I've learned that I *can* make a rational choice to overcome mere physical urges. My mind recognizes that you're the mate I need. The woman I can build a successful, satisfying life with. Anastasia could never be a true partner or a dependable parent. Not like you. In the end, raw physical passion is only temporary. Respect and affection are what make a marriage last." His eyes grew moist. "I want you back, Kate."

Two days ago she would have given anything to hear those words. Now they left her cold.

She wasn't sure exactly what had changed in the last forty-eight hours, but she knew that the relationship Chris was describing—the relationship he was willing to settle for—wasn't what she wanted anymore.

And she wasn't convinced it was what Chris wanted, either. What would happen if he met another woman like Anastasia—a woman who made him feel things Kate didn't?

"Let me be sure I have this straight," she said after a moment. "You fell for Anastasia because she was wild and adventurous—"

"Exactly. And the sex was like that, too."

Her hands clenched into fists. "Believe me, I haven't forgotten that point. But now you've decided the fact that I'm safe and predictable is actually a good thing, and you want us to get back together. Is that it?"

"Yes."

"And it won't be a problem that you don't enjoy sex with me as much as you enjoyed sex with her?"

He hesitated, as though recognizing that he was heading towards a quagmire with this one.

"I don't . . . That is . . . it's not that I don't enjoy sex with you, Kate. Of course I do. But it might not hurt to try some new things once in a while. You can be a little inhibited."

She nodded thoughtfully. "Maybe you could write down all the things Anastasia does that I don't do. Then you could do a point-by-point analysis."

Not even Chris could miss the bitterness in her voice that time.

He winced. "Okay, I get it. I should have been more diplomatic. But I think we need to be completely honest with each other if we're going to make things work between us."

The sound of her cell phone ringing stopped her from saying a few completely honest things right then and there.

"Excuse me a minute," she said to Chris, grabbing the phone from the coffee table and heading for the kitchen.

She didn't recognize the number on the screen, but she was so glad for the chance to cool down that she didn't care who was calling. Even a wrong number would be welcome.

"This is Kate Meredith."

"Hi, Kate. It's Ian."

Of course it was.

She slumped back against the refrigerator. "Why are you calling me, Hart? I don't have the time to deal with you right now. Believe it or not, you're currently the least of my worries."

"What's wrong?" he asked sharply. "You sound . . . Are you okay?"

She opened her mouth to deliver a stinging reply. Instead she heard herself say, "Chris is here."

"Chris? Who's that?"

"My fiancé. Sorry—ex-fiancé."

"Son of a bitch." A short silence. "What does he want?"

She should just hang up on him. It was a toss-up between Ian and Chris as to whom she hated more right now, and she had no reason in the world to continue this conversation.

But for some unaccountable reason, she did. "He wants us to get back together."

Another silence. "Is that what *you* want?"

"God, no." She took a deep breath. "He told me I'd make a better life partner than Anastasia, because I'm safe and predictable. Although he does think I should step up my game sexually. Try some new things once in a while." Her hand tightened on the phone. "Now that he has some basis for comparison."

As she heard herself say the words, she felt a rush of helpless anger. Maybe she and Chris hadn't set the sheets on fire, but he'd never told her he thought something was missing.

Instead of talking to her about it, he'd decided to sleep with another woman. And now that Anastasia was gone, he figured he might as well go back to Kate—especially if she could be more like Anastasia in bed.

"Son of a bitch," Ian said again. "He's still there?"

"Yes."

"Do you *want* him there?"

"No."

"Got it."

He disconnected the call, and Kate stared at the phone.

Well, that was weird. But when you balanced it against the weirdness sitting in her living room right now, it was hardly a drop in the bucket.

She wasn't ready to face Chris again just yet. She sat down at the kitchen table and put her head in her hands.

She didn't think it had been his intention, but Chris had triggered one of her deepest insecurities about herself.

He wasn't the first man who'd left her for someone more exciting. Adventurous. Whatever.

It wasn't an accident that she wrote about heroes and heroines who were brave, daring, confident, fearless—everything she wasn't. Even as a kid she'd been better at observing life than participating in it, and she'd always lived vicariously through the characters in stories—other people's at first, and then her own.

Her fictional heroines were larger than life. But she herself was small: timid, conventional, tame.

Boring.

A loud knock at the front door interrupted her pity party. She took a deep breath, ran her hands through her hair, and went back into the living room.

"Someone's at the door," Chris said helpfully.

Kate crossed the room, looked through the peephole, and froze.

It was Ian.

Not in his secret identity as Corporate Guy, but in his superhero identity as Tattooed Bad Boy.

He wasn't wearing any earrings this time, but he didn't need them. In his white tee shirt and jeans, with his stubbled jaw, tousled hair, and all that ink on full display, he looked as sexy and dangerous as any man she'd ever seen.

How had he gotten here so fast?

Maybe he really was a superhero. Tattooed Bad Boy, Defender of Jilted Women Everywhere.

She opened the door. "What are you—"

He stepped inside without waiting for an invitation. "Who the hell is this?" he asked, jerking his head towards Chris.

Chris got to his feet, looking bewildered, affronted, and a little alarmed. "I'm Kate's fiancé," he said stiffly. "Who the hell are *you*?"

Ian looked at her. "I think that's a question for Kate to answer," he said, his eyes making it clear that the ball was in her court. "Why don't you tell him who I am?"

She hesitated only a second. Then she lifted her chin and turned to face Chris.

"This is . . ." She groped for a bad-boy name. "Spike," she finished with satisfaction. "I met him at a club on Friday, and we hooked up."

Chris's jaw sagged open.

"You . . . he . . . *what*?"

She was starting to enjoy herself. "Yep, that's what happened. I guess I was feeling a little . . . spontaneous. You know how that is."

When she glanced at Ian, she saw his lips twitch.

He laid an arm over her shoulders. "I wanted to hook up with her last night, too, but I acted like an asshole and she walked out on me. I'm here to beg for forgiveness . . . and, God willing, to get laid."

She pretended to think about it. "Well . . ."

"I don't believe it," Chris said, his voice trembling. He took a few steps towards them. "You'd never hook up with a stranger—especially one like *him*. Tell me this is some kind of joke."

"He doesn't believe us," Ian murmured. When she looked up at him, she caught a wicked gleam in his eyes. "What can we do to prove it to him?"

She could think of no way to answer that question. "Um . . ."

He took her by the shoulders and pushed her back against the wall. Her eyes widened and her lips parted, but she didn't make a sound.

He leaned in close, his hands still gripping her upper arms. "What if I take you right here? Do you think that would convince him?"

His voice was low and raspy and intimate, and she could feel heat coming off his body.

Her heart was pounding and her mouth was dry. Ian's eyes, only inches away, glinted with amusement and something more.

Desire.

"Kate! We haven't finished our conversation. Tell this man to leave your apartment."

She was vaguely aware that Chris was speaking, but she couldn't have repeated his actual words to save her life. She was conscious only of Ian—his scent, his big body crowding hers, his hands on her shoulders, and the heat of his gaze.

She couldn't look away from him. Warmth flooded her face, and she could feel her cheeks turning red. Ian Hart was watching her blush like a teenager.

When she licked her dry lips, he followed the movement of her tongue with his eyes.

A wave of lust made her shiver. His hands tightened on her, and all she could think about was what they would feel like on the rest of her body.

"Kate. Kate!"

She turned her head and saw Chris standing a few feet from them. He looked furious.

She couldn't seem to form words. She looked back at Ian instead.

"Listen, buddy," he said. He was talking to Chris, but his eyes never left hers. "You can stay and watch if that's your thing, but if it's not, I suggest you get the hell out right now."

Chris stiffened. "Is that what you want, Kate? Do you want me to leave?"

Kate struggled back to rationality with an effort. "I think—" Her voice sort of croaked, and she cleared her throat. "I think that would be best."

One corner of Ian's mouth lifted. He lifted his hands from her shoulders to slide them into her hair, and her scalp prickled with delicious sensation.

"Fine," Chris said coldly. "But once you come to your senses, we have a lot to talk about."

"Mm-hmm," she murmured, barely paying attention. The door slammed shut behind him.

He was gone. Chris was gone.

Which meant that Ian had no reason to brush his thumbs over her cheekbones like that, and she had no reason to let her eyes drift closed.

He leaned even closer. "Kate," he whispered, his mouth so close that she shivered again.

She had to put a stop to this.

"Ian," she said, intending to speak firmly and decisively, using her voice to cut through this crazy sexual tension.

But his name came out in a breathy whisper.

~

When Ian had woken up that morning, he'd felt like crap. It hadn't taken long to figure out why.

He owed Kate an apology, and he wouldn't feel right until he gave it to her.

It didn't help that Jacob raved about her all through breakfast, talking more than he had in months. A little while later Maggie, a neighbor's daughter who watched Jacob on Sundays while Ian went to the gym, knocked on the door.

This was his chance. Telling Jacob he'd be back in a couple of hours, he headed for Kate's.

The doorman recognized him and let him into the building. He thought about going straight up to her apartment but hesitated in the lobby.

Maybe she'd tell him to go to hell, but he should still call first. She wouldn't appreciate his showing up at her door unannounced.

When she answered the phone her voice was tense and unhappy, and at first he thought he might be the cause. Then he found out the real reason.

Hearing that her asshole ex-fiancé was up there made him see red.

On his way up to her apartment, he pulled off his sweatshirt and messed up his hair a little. The fact that he hadn't shaved this morning would help with his bad-boy persona.

He wasn't sure if Kate needed a bad boy—or if she needed his help at all. But if she did, he'd be there.

He left it up to her. When she took the ball he tossed her and ran with it, he felt a rush of satisfaction. The loser who could dump Kate Meredith for another woman didn't deserve a single second of her time, and the sooner he got out of her apartment—and her life—the better. It was a pleasure to help out by playing the part of Spike, the rebound fling who'd showed Kate a very good time on Friday night.

Then he got a little carried away.

How the hell could he not? Kate looked so beautiful and vulnerable as she faced down her ex. She made him wish he had a white horse, so he could pull her up behind him and gallop off into the sunset.

Then the asshole was gone, and the time for playacting was over. He still had an apology to make to this woman, and he had no business crowding her against the wall, wishing she was wearing a skirt.

Although it was probably a good thing she wasn't. Because then he'd have to rely on his willpower to keep from unzipping his jeans, shoving her panties aside, and driving himself into her right here. And his willpower was starting to feel like a weak reed.

When she whispered his name, he shuddered.

He didn't have a chance. She was so close, so sexy, so responsive. A meteor hurtling towards Earth couldn't have stopped him from tilting her face up to his.

When their mouths met, a bolt of lightning went from his lips to his groin. She was so soft, so sweet . . . When her body arched in surrender, his own body felt hot and hard and arrogantly male.

Her lips parted and his tongue slid inside, thrusting against hers in a deliberately carnal rhythm. His hands moved down her body, brushing against the sides of her breasts before settling on her hips. Through a haze of lust he realized he was grinding into her, his erection rubbing against her belly in slow, explicit circles.

Then he realized that Kate's hands were on his shoulders—not to pull him closer but in an effort to push him away.

Damn.

He took a step back and turned his head away for a moment, giving them both a chance to recover.

When he heard Kate clear her throat, he risked looking back at her. Her cheeks were flushed and her lips were swollen.

"I just realized that Chris is gone," she said shakily. "So . . . you know . . . mission accomplished. No need to keep on . . ." Her voice trailed off, and she cleared her throat again. "In short, well done. You did a good job there. Thank you."

It was hard to sound calm and collected with an iron-hard erection straining against his jeans, but he did the best he could.

"No problem. Glad to help. That guy's a dick, by the way. You deserve a lot better."

"Thank you." She paused. "But speaking of dickish behavior . . ."

"Right." It was his turn to clear his throat. "I came here to apologize, as a matter of fact. But before I get to that, would you mind if I use your bathroom?"

"Of course. I mean, of course not. It's down the hall on the right."

He made his way there as casually as he could, even though it felt like his crotch was outlined in neon.

Once inside the bathroom with the door closed, he leaned over the sink and took a deep breath. Then he turned on the cold water and splashed his face.

Okay, that was better. The bulge in his jeans had subsided a little, and he no longer felt like a savage.

As he glanced around for a hand towel, he noticed that Kate had a nice bathroom. The walls were sage green, the crown molding and other trim done in a darker green. The rug on the floor was the color of sea foam. There were framed pictures on the wall, black-and-white drawings that looked vaguely familiar.

They were Edward Gorey's, he realized after a moment. Charming and whimsical.

The room smelled nice, too. As he finished drying his hands and face and hung the towel back on its hook, he noticed a basket of potpourri and caught the scent of cinnamon and roses.

He left the bathroom and headed back into the living room. He'd barely noticed his surroundings before, but now he took the time to look around at Kate's apartment.

It was a riot of color, but there was nothing discordant or strident. The walls were filled with paintings and photographs and prints, including one of a sword-wielding heroine captioned with the name Red Sonja. Not far from that bright splash of comic-book art, a beautiful quilt in shades of blue and lavender hung above the mantelpiece.

None of the furniture matched, but somehow it all went together. There was a lot of wood in different tones—cherry, mahogany, ebony—and the seating ranged from leather armchairs to antique rockers to an overstuffed sofa upholstered in pale peach fabric, with throw pillows in every shade of orange—pumpkin, apricot, tangerine.

It smelled good in here, too. Fresh and sweet. He didn't notice any potpourri, but there were terra cotta pots filled with lush greenery and vases of flowers—roses, tulips, daffodils.

The hardwood floors glowed with the honeyed patina given by decades of care. There were books and bookcases everywhere, antique leather bindings side by side with comic books and thrillers. The lamps were as eclectic as everything else—ceramic, wood, and metal bases paired with every kind of shade, including Tiffany-style stained glass. There were wooden blinds on the windows instead of curtains, and the shafts of sunlight filtering through the slats made geometric patterns on the walls and floors.

All in all, it was one of the most appealing and inviting interior spaces he'd ever been in. He started to say so, but then he remembered her comment the night before about his "soulless palace of luxury" and a flicker of annoyance made him hold back the compliment.

Instead, he nodded towards the window seat, where a black-and-white feline was curled up, asleep. "Is that the cat you told Jacob about?"

Kate looked like she'd taken advantage of his short absence to compose herself. She'd redone her ponytail and straightened her clothing—black yoga pants and a gray thermal top—and her face, though still glowing, was no longer flushed.

She nodded. "Yes, that's him."

"What's his name again?"

"Gallifrey."

"Right. From *Doctor Who*." Wanting to show that he wasn't ignorant about shows on other networks, he went on. "I've been impressed by the way the BBC has driven its popularity in the US. Social media, home DVD sales, product tie-ins . . ."

He stopped when he saw the look on her face. "What?"

She shook her head. "Do you want to know why *Doctor Who* is so popular?"

"Go ahead and tell me, Miss Know-It-All," he said, but there was no rancor in his voice.

She grinned at him. "Because it's wonderful. Creative, exciting, funny, and full of heart."

"So no credit goes to the marketing and publicity teams, huh?"

"I suppose they deserve a little credit. But they had a great product to work with." She paused. "Not that this isn't fun, but I think you mentioned something about an apology?"

"Yeah." He paused. "I was a jerk to you last night, and I'm sorry. I had no right to speak to you like that, especially when—as you pointed out—you'd spent the last several hours babysitting for me. I guess it's obvious that I'm a little defensive where my nephew is concerned. Losing his mother was hard on both of us, and it's important to me to do right by him."

When she sat down in one of the armchairs, he took a seat on the couch. She tucked her bare feet under her, and that, along with her ponytail, made her look much younger than she was.

"Does this mean you'll actually think about what I said?"

He shook his head. "We'll have to agree to disagree about Jacob and sports. I don't think there's anything wrong with the person he is, but I want him to broaden his horizons a little."

Kate opened her mouth and he held up a hand. "In the interest of détente, I suggest we drop the subject."

She hesitated a moment and then nodded. "Fair enough. Do you have any ideas for a new topic?"

"Two. First, if you still want a date to your friend's wedding, I hope you'll let me take you."

She looked thoughtful. "Can I let you know in a few days?"

"Of course. The second thing is actually a favor."

Her eyebrows went up. "Another favor?"

"It's actually the same one—or a continuation of it."

"Meaning?"

"During this time of transition—"

"For which I have you to thank—"

"I wondered if you would consider watching Jacob a couple of times a week."

There was a short silence. "I have to be honest, Hart—I'm a little surprised that you're asking me. Our relationship isn't too amicable, and my last babysitting gig for you didn't end well."

"That's a fair point." He paused. "The truth is, it was Jacob's idea. The woman who's been watching him Tuesdays and Fridays—the same woman who was supposed to watch him yesterday—isn't available anymore. We were talking about it this morning, and Jacob suggested that I ask you about it. Of course I told him you might not be able to," he added quickly. "But if you could do it—even for just a few weeks—well, I think it would mean a lot to him. He's usually so quiet, and this morning he couldn't stop talking about you. It was nice to see him so animated." He paused again. "Of course, since this would be a more regular arrangement, I'd pay you whatever you—"

"Will you stop with the money thing? If I agree to help you out, it'll be because Jacob's a nice kid and I enjoy his company."

He frowned. "I don't know if I'm comfortable with that. You're unemployed, and you'd be providing a service. You should be paid for your time."

"It's very nice of you to worry about my finances," she said drily. "But I have enough in savings to make it through this 'time of transition.' And even if I didn't, I was born with a silver spoon in my mouth, right? You can't think my parents would let their spoiled princess struggle."

He winced. "Okay, fine, I deserved that. Do you need me to apologize again?"

"I think once is enough. And I'd be glad to watch Jacob on Tuesdays and Fridays, at least for a while."

Relief swept through him. "That's great. I really appreciate it, Kate."

When had this started to matter so much? It wasn't like the world would come to an end if his nephew didn't see Kate again.

Or if he didn't.

Ian glanced around her living room before he let his gaze return to her. With her legs tucked under her like that and a few soft curls escaping from her ponytail, she looked as warm and inviting as her apartment.

It dawned on him that his relief was as much for his own sake as for Jacob's. Because he did want to see her again.

75

Three days ago, Kate Meredith had been on his top-ten list of people to avoid. They'd rubbed each other the wrong way from the moment they'd met, and even though he'd felt bad about cancelling her show, he hadn't felt bad that he wouldn't be seeing her again.

Now, just seventy-two hours later, the idea of Kate disappearing from his life was unacceptable.

He remembered the kiss against her wall, and his body tightened.

Who would have guessed that head-in-the-clouds Kate Meredith had that kind of sexual fire inside her? He'd never suspected it—and it was obvious her idiot ex-fiancé had never touched that part of her.

Maybe nobody had.

His body tightened again. The thought was unexpectedly arousing.

He could reach that part of her. He could take her places she'd never dreamed of.

Was it so crazy to think that the two of them might get together? Not right away, of course—she'd just broken up with her fiancé. But after a month, or even a few weeks . . .

Of course they'd have to be sure that whatever happened between them didn't affect Jacob. When things ended, it would be important to end them amicably.

The more he thought about it, the more the idea appealed to him. They'd never work as a couple; they were too different, and he didn't do relationships. But why couldn't he be her rebound guy? Her friend Simone had said she needed to cut loose. Maybe she could do that with him.

The idea of cutting loose with Kate kicked his pulse into high gear.

Come to think of it, they had all the necessary qualifications for a classic fling—off-the-charts chemistry and no long-term potential. And when he remembered the way Kate had responded to his kiss, it was hard to believe she'd say no. Hadn't she said Friday night that she wanted a bad boy she could use for sex?

She could use him for sex anytime she wanted.

"There is one thing I think we should address," Kate said.

Great—she was going to bring up the sports thing again. He steeled himself for an argument.

"Shoot."

Kate shifted her position in the chair, untucking her feet and crossing her legs. "I'm sure this goes without saying, but I think it's important that we avoid any encounters like . . . well . . . what happened when Chris was here. Of course, there's no reason to think anything like that would happen again," she added quickly. "But I thought we should, you know, establish that formally."

"Establish it formally," Ian repeated.

She nodded. "Yes. To make it clear we're not going to cross that line. Not that we would, of course. It's not like we're really attracted to each other or anything. Friday night we were both drinking, and today you were just helping me out with Chris. But I thought we should make it clear."

"I see."

He didn't say anything else, and as the silence stretched out, Kate's cheeks turned pink.

"I'm not saying I didn't appreciate your, um, help. With Chris. But since we're not, as I said, really attracted to each other . . ." Her voice trailed off.

Did Kate honestly believe that? Or was it just something she needed to say for her own peace of mind?

When he realized he was pissed off, he got even more pissed off. What the hell did it matter to him if Kate wanted to pretend there was no chemistry between them? If he was in the mood for a fling, there was no shortage of willing women in Manhattan. He sure as hell didn't need to go after this one.

"Good point," he said, getting to his feet. "Well, then. You're sure you don't mind watching Jacob?"

Kate stood, too, looking relieved. "It'll be my pleasure. Give me a call later, and we'll work out the details."

That was the real reason he'd come to see Kate—to apologize for last night and ask her to watch Jacob. He was here for his nephew's sake, not his. So, mission accomplished. Right?

He headed for the door and Kate came with him.

When he turned to say goodbye, he realized he was still pissed off . . . and turned on. It was an unsettling combination.

"Is everything all right?"

He frowned at her. "Of course. Why do you ask?"

"You're kind of . . . scowling."

Her words made him scowl more. "I'm fine," he said brusquely.

Another few curls had escaped her ponytail. They made a kind of aureole around her face, and that, along with her rosy cheeks and big blue eyes, made her look sweet and innocent.

But he knew, now, the fire that lay behind that innocence.

Before he could stop himself, he reached out and tucked one of those coppery curls behind her ear.

He was pretty sure he'd never noticed a woman's ears before, since he was usually focused on more traditionally appealing attributes. But now he found himself staring at Kate's.

They were as perfectly formed as the rest of her, with a translucent, shell-like delicacy. She flushed under his gaze, and because he was standing close, he could watch the progress of the heat that crept into her face, staining that perfect skin with a rosy glow.

Her earlobes turned pink, and it took a real effort of will not to close his teeth over one.

His eyes met hers. "It's a good thing we're not attracted to each other," he said. "Because otherwise, I might misinterpret that blush."

It was her turn to scowl. "I'm not blushing."

The lie was so blatant that he couldn't resist trying to make her blush even more. He tucked another curl behind her ear, and this time he let his hand linger, tracing the line of her ear with a fingertip. Then he trailed his fingers down the side of her neck.

Her breath came faster, and her cheeks were so red she looked as if she'd been hiking in the Alps.

"Yeah, you're not blushing at all," he said, his voice low and intimate as his eyes locked on hers again. "My mistake."

Then he backed off, giving her a smile as he opened the door. "I'll call you in a few days about Jacob. Take care, Kate."

A minute later, heading down to the lobby, Ian wondered why he still felt unsettled—and why he wasn't feeling more satisfaction at having made Kate blush like that. Then he caught sight of his reflection in the metal wall of the elevator.

Maybe it was because if Kate had looked down, she would have noticed that his body was reacting just as powerfully as hers.

Chapter Five

"So, Kate . . . tell us about this rebound fling of yours."

That was Jessica, her eyes alight with curiosity. When Kate glanced around the table at the other women sitting there, she saw avid interest but no surprise—which meant that Jessica had already informed them of Kate's supposed adventures.

Of course she had.

Simone, sitting on her left, chimed in. "Yeah, Kate, tell us. We're all agog."

Kate kicked Simone's ankle before smiling at the other six bridesmaids. It was Thursday, which meant that they were at the Ritz-Carlton having afternoon tea, a ritual Jessica had instituted a few months ago. She used this weekly meeting as a chance to go over wedding-planning details, to talk about her latest hair and makeup ideas for The Day, and, of course, to gossip.

"There's not much to tell," Kate said, going for a blasé tone—the tone of a woman who ate men like Ian Hart for breakfast.

But then she flashed back to the kiss in her apartment, and her lips tingled from the memory of Ian's hot, hard, demanding mouth.

She felt her face heating up as she continued. "It was just a hookup. No big deal."

Jessica looked at her in exasperation. "At least give us some details. What does he look like, for starters?"

"I can tell you that much," Simone said smugly. "I've met him."

This elicited a chorus of questions from the bridesmaids.

"What's he like?"

"What's his name?"

"Is he hot? I bet he's hot."

"'Hot' doesn't begin to describe it," Simone said, giving Kate a sideways grin. Kate attempted to shoot daggers with her eyes, but like so many other great metaphors, it wasn't possible in real life.

Simone leaned back and crossed her legs. She made an interesting contrast with the elegantly brocaded armchair, dressed as she was in black leather and combat boots.

"He's tall and built like a mixed-martial-arts fighter. He's got the kind of upper body that makes you imagine him in bed, supporting his weight with his arms . . . the way his chest and shoulders and biceps would be all rock-hard, you know? Not to mention other parts of him. His face is rugged—firm jaw, sexy cheekbones, the whole package. He's got green eyes and black hair. His arms are covered in these gorgeous tattoos—"

"Tattoos? He's got tattoos?" Jessica sounded intrigued and titillated.

"Yep."

In spite of herself, Kate couldn't help feeling a little pleased at the reactions of the other women. She was so used to being the one with no wild escapades or tales of seduction to share.

The truth was, it was kind of fun to be seen as a woman who could bag a sexy bad boy. But it was probably time to change the subject. "Okay, I think that's enough about my rebound fling. Jessica, weren't you going to tell us something about our dresses? You said it was urgent," Kate reminded her.

Jessica wavered a moment, torn between the salacious details of Kate's adventure and the overmastering importance of anything related to her wedding.

The wedding won out, as Kate had known it would.

"Well," Jessica said, leaning forward, "I had an inspiration. As some of you know, my sister has never been thrilled with her bridesmaid dress."

"It makes me look like a Twinkie shrink-wrapped in cellophane," Vicki said.

Kate hid a smile. She'd always liked Vicki, who never hesitated to speak her mind.

Jessica rolled her eyes. "Anyway, I was talking with the people at Rosalind's, and they said they could scrap the original design and make everyone brand-new dresses from scratch."

"For a small fortune," Vicki added. "A fortune that could be better used to fund a hospital wing or something like that. But since I no longer have to look like a sausage about to burst its skin, I'm all for it. Although I am making a large donation to cancer research out of guilt."

Maria, a childhood friend of Jessica's, shook her head slowly. "I can't believe you're changing the bridesmaid dresses this close to the wedding. Are you sure they'll be done on time?"

Vicki snorted. "Considering the size of the check our father gave them, they could afford to construct a time machine to give them any extra cushion they might need."

That was actually a pretty cool idea.

"A time machine for a dressmaker," Kate mused. "I love it. You could do a modern retelling of the Cinderella story with the fairy godmother as a—"

"Please don't do that thing right now," Jessica interrupted.

"What thing?"

"That turning-everything-into-a-story thing. This is real life, remember?"

Right, real life. Which, as always, was sadly inferior to Kate's imagination.

"There is one thing I need you all to do," Jessica went on. "Rosalind's scheduled us for a fitting tomorrow night, so—"

"No can do," Simone put in. "I have to be at the theater to meet the new director."

"I have plans, too," Kate said. "I'm babysitting."

"Babysitting?" Jessica looked flummoxed for a moment, then perked up almost immediately. "That's no problem. You can bring her along."

"It's a him, and I can't drag an eleven-year-old boy to a dress fitting."

Jessica waved her objection away. "If he's got a Nintendo or whatever, and if he's anything like Heather's kids, he won't even notice where he is."

Heather herself spoke up. "Speaking of my kids—and believe me, they're the only reason I know this—there's a comic book store right next to Rosalind's. That might tempt him."

Kate thought about it. She knew the store Heather was talking about—it was a geek paradise.

"Well . . . I'm supposed to pick up Jacob after school tomorrow. I'll check with him, and if he's okay with it, I'll let you know. That's the best I can do."

Jessica looked at Simone. "What about you? When are you meeting your director?"

"Eight o'clock."

"That shouldn't be a problem. The fitting is at six. My driver can take you to the theater afterwards."

Simone shook her head. "There's a kind of insouciant greatness to your noblesse oblige."

Jessica made a face. "As usual, I haven't the faintest idea what you're talking about. Is that a yes, or what?"

"Oh, I suppose so. Might as well get it over with."

"Great." Jessica wore the satisfied expression of a bride who's just gotten her way. "We'll meet at Rosalind's at six. It'll be fabulous."

Fabulous.

∽

The next afternoon was as perfect as only a few days in May ever are. When Kate met Jacob in front of his school, which turned out to be ten blocks south of her apartment, she asked how he wanted to get home.

"We can take a cab if you like, but it will only take twenty minutes to walk across the park. Of course, it'll be a little longer if we stop to get pretzels on the way."

"Let's walk!" he said immediately, and Kate couldn't have agreed more.

A little while later, when they were sitting on a bench eating their pretzels, Kate told Jacob about the fitting.

"I promised my friend I'd ask you about it, but if you don't want to go, that's okay." She popped the last bit of pretzel into her mouth. "I was told to mention, though, that Ezra's Entertainment is right next door to the boutique. Have you ever been there?"

Jacob shook his head, his cheeks bulging with the enormous bite he'd just taken.

"It's one of the best comic stores in the city. They have posters and tee shirts and games, too. We can hang out there until it's my turn to try something on."

Jacob had to finish chewing before he could answer. "Sure, that sounds great. I'd go even if it wasn't next to a comic store. I can always bring a book or my tablet or whatever."

Kate grinned at him. "You're a pretty decent kid, you know that? In spite of the fact that you enjoyed the *Star Wars* prequels and have never watched the classic episodes of *Doctor Who*. These are faults of youth and can therefore be forgiven."

Jacob rolled his eyes, but he'd taken another bite of pretzel and was too busy chewing to answer.

Her phone rang, and she fished it out of her purse. When she saw it was Ian, a little jolt went through her system.

She wished that would stop happening. When he'd called earlier in the week to ask if she could watch Jacob today, her heart had jumped as if she were a teenager hearing from the cutest boy in class. After the call had ended, she'd found herself singing "I Feel Pretty" from *West Side Story*.

For a grown woman, that was downright embarrassing. Especially considering she'd made such a point of establishing that nothing was going to happen between them—not to mention their lack of attraction for each other.

Yeah, right.

The truth was, she didn't think she'd ever been as attracted to a man as she was to Ian Hart. Until now, she hadn't known she could feel that way about a man she didn't even like.

Unless it was *because* she didn't like him.

Well, why not? If you imagined yourself with a guy you didn't like, emotion wouldn't enter into it. There'd be no girlish dreams of happily-ever-after.

Just raw, primitive, mind-blowing sex.

Not that she would ever fantasize about Ian, of course.

She got up from the bench before she took his call. She felt more in control when she was on her feet, and with Ian Hart she needed every possible advantage.

"Hey," she said.

"Hey, yourself. Any problems picking up Jacob?"

She tried to ignore her body's response to the whiskey-rough timbre of his voice. "Not at all. It's such a gorgeous day we decided to walk home, and we're currently eating soft pretzels in Central Park."

"Must be nice. I just came out of a meeting and I'm on my way to another one. I haven't been outside all day."

"Poor baby. Of course the fact that you're gainfully employed is probably some consolation."

"I offered to gainfully employ you, remember? You were the one who insisted on doing this out of the goodness of your heart."

"I wanted to show you that some people actually have one."

He chuckled. "I have a heart. It's just two sizes too small."

Her eyebrows rose. "A Dr. Seuss reference? I'm impressed. I didn't know you had it in you."

"Yeah, I've noticed your tendency to underestimate me."

When she realized their back-and-forth was making her smile, she decided it was time to change the subject. "I'm actually glad you called. I need to check with you about something."

She told him about the fitting that evening and Jacob's offer to come with her. "We wouldn't be back late—probably around eight or eight thirty. It's not a school night, but even so, if you'd rather he stayed home, I completely understand. It wouldn't break my heart to skip a fitting with Bridezilla."

"No, you should go. And I might be able to get you out a little early, if it's okay with your friend—and if you're amenable."

"You could suggest anything to get me out early, up to and including helping you bury a body, and I'd be amenable."

He chuckled again. "A friend of mine has three tickets to the Yankees game tonight and can't use them. They're fantastic seats, field level on the third-base line. I know you're not a sports fan, but I thought you might—"

"They're playing the Red Sox tonight," she interrupted.

"You know that? I'm impressed. I wouldn't have thought you'd know the first thing about the Yankees' schedule."

"Yeah, I've noticed your tendency to underestimate me."

"Funny girl. So does this mean you're actually a Yankees fan?"

"Not even a little bit."

"I guess that was too much to hope for. But what about going to the game tonight? Are you interested? Or is sitting through three hours of baseball your idea of torture?"

"Let me check with my partner in crime." She'd walked a few paces away during their conversation, and now she turned back towards Jacob as she lowered the phone. "How would you feel about going to a Yankees game tonight?"

His forehead wrinkled. "Well . . . are you going to be there?"

"Yes."

"Then sure."

She lifted the phone again. "We're on, Hart."

"Great. First pitch is at 7:05, but we'll have to be a little late, since I can't leave work until six thirty. Will it be okay with your friend if I pick you and Jacob up at seven? That'll get us to the stadium by the second inning."

"Absolutely. I'll text you the address of the boutique, and we'll be waiting out front at seven sharp."

After the call ended, she and Jacob started walking again. She didn't realize she was grinning until Jacob said, "You look happy. I guess you really like baseball, huh? I don't understand why people love it so much. I think it's totally boring."

"That's because no one ever made it into a story for you."

"A story? What do you mean?"

"Pull up a chair, Jacob—metaphorically speaking. I'm going to tell you about the curse of the Bambino."

"There's a curse involved? That does sound cool."

"It is. Would you mind if we take a detour to my apartment? There's something I'd like to pick up for tonight."

"Will I be able to meet Gallifrey?"

"Of course. He's always happy to acquire new admirers."

∼

Ian cut his last meeting short and headed out the door at six fifteen. He told himself he was excited because of Jacob, not Kate. This would be another chance to get his nephew into sports.

Although, come to think of it, maybe he could use this opportunity to get Kate into sports, too. That would be an even bigger challenge, considering how closed-minded she could be.

But he was always up for a challenge.

He arrived at the address Kate had sent him at six forty-five. He'd told her seven, so he didn't want to rush her, but if she was finished with her fitting she might appreciate the chance to leave early.

It was Jacob who answered her phone. "Kate lent it to me so I could play a game," he explained.

"That was nice of her. I'm calling because I got out of work early and I'm out front now. There's no hurry, but you guys can leave whenever Kate's finished."

"She's trying on her dress, so we can't go yet." There was a short pause. "You want to know something weird?"

"Sure."

"The girls in my class can be really mean to each other, you know? But I always figured they'd grow out of that eventually—like, by the time they go to college or whatever. But Kate's friends are grown-ups and they're still mean. Well, not all of them. Her friend Simone is awesome. But the bride made Kate feel bad a bunch of times."

Ian's hand tightened on the phone. "How?"

"She's little, like Simone, and she makes jokes about how tall Kate is. She said guys like to feel big when they stand next to a woman, and she said maybe that's why Kate has trouble hanging onto a man. Then she sort of smiled and said, 'Just kidding.' Kate didn't say anything, but I could tell her feelings were hurt."

Ian was surprised at the rush of protective anger that went through him. "Listen, Jacob—I'm coming in. Will you meet me by the front door?"

"Sure."

He was wearing his Yankees sweatshirt, but he had a tee shirt on underneath it. Wondering how many times in his association with Kate Meredith he was going to take off his clothes, he pulled off the sweatshirt, messed up his hair, and told the driver he'd be out in a few minutes.

Jacob was waiting for him just inside the door, and his eyes widened when he saw his uncle. "You never wear short sleeves in public. And your hair looks different."

"I know. Would you mind waiting in the car while I get Kate?"

"Sure, but she's not ready to go yet. She's still got the dress on."

"I'll wait until she's ready."

"Okay."

Ian watched through the glass doors until Jacob was in the car. Then he went to find Kate.

She was in one of the back rooms. The doors were all marked private, but when he heard a gaggle of female voices behind one of them, he opened it.

The room he found himself in was small and elegant and smelled like perfume. The women were gathered around a kind of pedestal in the middle of the floor, some standing and some sitting on little gilt chairs, talking with each other and looking at the woman currently on display.

It was Kate.

She was wearing what he figured was her bridesmaid's dress for the wedding from hell. If so, the denizens of the lower regions were a lot better dressed then he'd previously imagined.

Ian didn't know that much about women's clothes, but he knew what he liked. Or maybe it would be more accurate to say that he liked Kate.

The way she *looked*. He liked the way Kate *looked*.

For the last two years he'd seen her only in her work clothes, which were pretty uninspired. Seeing her in her vamp outfit last week had been a revelation, and he'd enjoyed seeing her in jeans the next day and yoga pants the day after that.

But this . . .

He'd been to more red-carpet events than he could count, and in this dress Kate could stand shoulder to shoulder with any actress he'd ever seen.

It was chartreuse, which was not a color he'd ever expected to drool over. But it was the perfect complement to Kate's fair skin and red hair.

The material was satin, or maybe silk—something shiny, anyway—and it had a high neck and short sleeves and was slit up the side. More importantly, it outlined Kate's bodacious body with loving fidelity.

His jaw sagged when he first saw her, but by the time she noticed him he'd closed his mouth and was looking less like a demented schoolboy.

Kate's eyes widened when she spotted him. "I thought we were meeting out front," she said pointedly, her cheeks turning pink.

That got everyone's attention, and he found himself being stared at by every woman in the room, including one who was little and blonde and sat in her chair like a queen holding court.

Bridezilla, he presumed.

"I know," he said. "But I had to check you out in your fancy dress. And I'm glad I did," he added, letting his eyes move down her body and back up to her face.

A little blatant ogling was in character, right?

"You look like every man's fantasy in that thing," he went on. Then he turned towards the little blonde. "Are you the bride?"

"Yes," she said, rising to her feet and coming towards him. "I'm Jessica," she added, holding out her hand and flashing a smile.

"I'm Spike," he said, catching Simone's sudden grin out of the corner of his eye. "I've got to say, I admire your courage."

"My courage?"

"Yeah. I thought the idea was to make your bridesmaids look hideous, so you look even better in comparison. You must have a lot of self-confidence to let Kate walk down the aisle looking like that."

"Thank you," Jessica said after a moment, her voice a little stiff. She dropped his hand and turned her back on him, and Ian took the opportunity to return Simone's wink.

"Well, ladies, I'll leave you to it." He looked at Kate again. "See you out front, babe."

He left the room without waiting for a response, smiling to himself as he shut the door behind him.

She came out of the boutique about ten minutes later, but he didn't recognize her at first. Her red hair was tucked under a baseball cap, and she was wearing—

He peered out the car window. "You've got to be kidding me."

Jacob grinned. "Yeah, Kate's a Red Sox fan. Didn't you know?"

Of course she was. It made perfect cosmic sense.

She opened the car door and slid in next to Jacob. "Hi," she said brightly, smiling at him under the brim of her ancient cap.

The state of that cap told him that she hadn't dressed like this just to annoy him. That cap, along with her faded jersey, spoke of many, many years of rooting for Boston.

He sighed and spoke to the driver. "Okay, Dave—take us to Yankee Stadium."

Dave grinned at him in the rearview mirror and pulled away from the curb.

Ian shook his head. "I thought you were a New Yorker," he said to Kate.

"I'm a transplant. My mother's a New Yorker, but my dad's from Boston. That's where I grew up."

"Is your mother a Yankees fan, at least?"

She shook her head. "Mets."

"Figures."

He'd never pegged Kate as any kind of sports fan—but he'd obviously been wrong.

"I'm excited for the game," Jacob said, and Ian stared at him.

"You are?"

"Uh-huh. Kate's been telling me all about the Red Sox. Fenway Park and selling Babe Ruth and Ted Williams and Carlton Fisk's home run and the ball between Bill Buckner's legs and the 2004 ALCS when they were down three games to none against the Yankees and the Yankees still managed to lose the series. She said it was the worst choke in sports history."

He glared at Kate, who was looking smug. "If you turn my nephew into a Red Sox fan, I will hold you morally and legally responsible."

"That decision is entirely up to him. I'm just giving him the information he needs to make an informed choice."

"Life's a lot easier in this town when you root for the Yankees."

"True—and Jacob is certainly entitled to take that into consideration as he ponders his options."

It took them only twenty minutes to get to the stadium. On their way to their seats Jacob stopped to use the bathroom, and as soon as the door closed behind him Kate poked Ian in the ribs.

"So, are you going to tell me why Spike made an appearance at my dress fitting?"

Was she grateful that he'd been there? Annoyed? He couldn't tell from her expression.

He shrugged. "Jacob answered your phone when I called. He said the bride was acting like one of the mean girls in his class."

That made her laugh. "That's funny . . . and true."

"He was afraid she'd hurt your feelings."

Her expression softened. "Jacob's a sweet kid."

He raised a brow. "I'm the one who went in there, you know."

"And?"

"Doesn't that make me sweet, too?"

It was blatant fishing, but he couldn't seem to help himself. A part of him wanted to hear her say "my hero" or something equally ridiculous.

She grinned at him. "I guess it *was* pretty sweet . . . even though I can hold my own with the mean girls of the world. I've been this height since I was twelve years old, so I've had a lot of practice. It's not easy being the tallest girl in class."

"I think you're the perfect height."

Once again, he couldn't help himself. She looked so damn cute in that baseball cap . . . and so damn sexy in that jersey. It was a struggle not to let his eyes drop to where her curves stretched the faded lettering across her chest.

It was her turn to raise a brow. "The perfect height for what?"

Was she flirting with him? Considering that it had been less than a week since she'd "formally established" that they wouldn't be crossing any lines, he considered this a minor triumph.

But he didn't show it. If he really wanted to get Kate into his bed, he couldn't move too fast. He had to—

Wait a second. He'd decided last week that seducing Kate Meredith would be more trouble than it was worth. When had he changed his mind about that?

Looking into her blue eyes, he decided it didn't matter. The fact was, he did want her in his bed. And if that would require more finesse than he usually needed with a woman, well, then, so be it.

So he just said, "The perfect height in general." Then he changed the subject. "Do you mind if I ask you a personal question?"

"Go ahead."

"Why in the world are you friends with that woman?"

Kate laughed. "Everyone who meets Jessica asks that question."

"So what's the answer?"

"Well . . . I've known her since college. I know she seems bitchy—and sometimes she really is. But a lot of that is a defense mechanism. When she was younger, she . . ." Kate paused. "You don't need to hear about that," she went on after a moment. "But I'll tell you something she did once. The summer after our junior year, my grandmother passed away. Jessica was in Monte Carlo with her family, but when she found out, she flew back and spent three weeks with me. She didn't say anything about it—she just moved in and took care of everything. My grandmother and I were really close, and Jessica knew how hard it was for me to lose her. So even though she can be hard to take sometimes, underneath it all she has a good heart."

"Hmm. I guess you can't always tell about people, can you?"

A moment later, Jacob came out of the restroom and it was time to focus on baseball.

It was a gorgeous night. Ian couldn't remember ever having enjoyed a game so much—especially since the Yankees pulled out a win in the bottom of the ninth with a squeeze play at home plate.

He had to admit that Kate was the main reason they had so much fun. She drew Jacob into the action by making everything into a drama—the way the pitcher and batter stared each other down, the way a pinch runner took a lead off first and threw the pitcher off his game, the magic of an inning-ending double play in the fourth, and an inside-the-park home run in the seventh.

He'd started off by suggesting that Jacob score the game with him—something he'd tried before with no success—but Kate waved him off. He gave in readily enough, enjoying her play-by-play patter so much he forgot to mark up his own scorecard.

It wasn't until the eighth inning that he realized how much knowledge of the game she'd managed to impart along the way.

"Did you see the infield shift?" Jacob said excitedly. "They're going to try to get Hernandez to hit into a double play."

He'd never seen Jacob so enthusiastic. He was actually bouncing in his seat.

He caught Kate's eye over the boy's head, and she smiled at him.

It would have been physically impossible not to smile back. She had a streak of mustard on her chin, her jersey was covered with powdered sugar from her funnel cake, and she looked adorable.

Jacob talked a blue streak on the way back to Kate's apartment, and since Ian wasn't able to get a word in edgewise, he had plenty of time to remind himself that he shouldn't walk Kate upstairs tonight. The urge to kiss her would be too strong, and he didn't want to scare her off.

His resolution was aided by the fact that Jacob fell asleep against his shoulder a few minutes before they pulled up in front of Kate's building.

Kate climbed out of the car on her side and then came around to his, motioning for him to roll down his window.

"I had a great time tonight, Ian. Thanks for letting a Sox fan use one of your tickets."

After a week of being Hart, he was Ian again. That fact unexpectedly warmed him.

"I'm glad you had fun. Thanks for watching Jacob today, and for coming to the game with us. We had a great time, too."

The mustard was gone, and she'd brushed off most of the powdered sugar, but she was still adorable.

Then she leaned in and kissed him on the cheek. Her baseball cap fell off when it knocked against the window, and her hair came tumbling down, brushing against his face. For an instant he was surrounded by the scent of jasmine. Then she picked up her cap, backed away from the car, and waved goodbye.

His cheek still tingled where she'd kissed him.

Chapter Six

When Simone called the next day, she didn't waste time with pleasantries.

"I need you," she said as soon as Kate answered the phone. "Code red."

For Kate, a code-red catastrophe meant wine and a Joss Whedon marathon—preferably *Firefly*. For Simone, it meant chocolate and a trip to the Metropolitan Museum of Art.

Kate rolled onto her side and glanced at the clock. It was eight thirty.

"What are you doing up at this hour?" Simone usually partied until dawn on Friday nights and slept until noon the next day.

"I told you, I have a code red. Meet me on the steps at ten?"

"Will do."

The day was cloudy but warm, and Kate enjoyed the walk across Central Park. She left early and took her time, stopping on the way for two espressos. When she passed a group of kids playing baseball, she found herself smiling.

She got to the Met at five minutes to ten, but Simone was there before her, sitting with her arms wrapped around her knees and a scowl on her face.

Another indication of her emotional state was the fact that she was wearing jeans and sneakers and no makeup and hadn't done anything to her hair.

"I feel like I'm meeting my new roommate freshman year," Kate said as she came up the steps. "You look so sweet and innocent and guileless."

She handed Simone one of the espressos, which her friend downed in a few grateful gulps.

"I might not be sweet and innocent anymore, but I'm still guileless. If I had any guile, I would have figured a way out of going to Ireland this summer."

Kate sat down on the steps beside her. "You're going to Ireland? On a plane?"

Simone nodded glumly. "I can't take a boat—I won't have enough time between my work schedule here and the production schedule over there."

Simone was terrified of flying. Which, of course, begged the question, "Why on earth did you agree to work on a show in Ireland?"

Simone crumpled her empty espresso cup in her hands. "Do you mind if we go inside first? I need the House of Dior around me now."

Simone's equivalent of comfort food was the Met's Costume Institute exhibit.

Kate patted her on the shoulder. "Let's get you in there."

Walking through the costume wing was like walking through the tropical-bird room at a zoo: brilliant colors, gaudy jewels, and a bewildering variety of tones and textures. After half an hour, Kate and Simone sat down on a cushioned bench in front of an eighteenth-century French court dress.

Simone took a deep breath. "So, you know we have a visiting director from a British theater company?"

Kate nodded. Simone belonged to an experimental performance group and did everything from lighting design to set and production work, although costume design was her first love.

"We're doing *Twelfth Night* and *A Midsummer Night's Dream* here in New York, and then we're going to Ireland to perform there."

I didn't think they'd need me, but the director is insisting that the entire production team go along."

The lighting in this wing was dim, but even so, Kate couldn't miss the flush that stole into Simone's cheeks.

Interesting.

"This is the director you met for the first time last night?" She asked the question casually, but she was watching her friend like a hawk.

"That's right."

No doubt about it—the blush was deepening. Even Simone's ears were turning red.

"I think I need to hear more about this director."

Simone glanced at her sideways. "Why?"

"Because you're blushing like a schoolgirl, that's why."

"I am not."

"You absolutely are."

"Just because you have a crush on a guy doesn't mean that I—"

"Hey! I do not have a crush on a guy."

Simone rolled her eyes. "Oh, please. I was there at Rosalind's when 'Spike' came in. Talk about blushing like a schoolgirl. And that reminds me—how was the game? Did the Sox win?"

"They were ahead until the bottom of the ninth, when the Yankees scored three runs."

"And what about Ian?"

"What about him?"

"Did *he* score last night?"

It was Kate's turn to roll her eyes. "Very funny. And no."

Simone grinned. "Then what the hell is wrong with you? You need to hit that, girlfriend. Talk about a quality rebound."

"May I remind you that this is the man who cancelled my show?"

"So let him make it up to you. And anyway, hasn't he helped you out since then? If you ask me, you're just hanging onto the whole 'he cancelled my show' thing to avoid dealing with the fact that you have the hots for him."

Kate would have delivered a snappy comeback, but Simone was so unexpectedly on the mark that for a moment Kate was tongue-tied.

"I knew it," Simone said smugly. "You want to drag him into your cave and have your way with him."

Also on the mark.

"And about your show—weren't you telling me just a few weeks ago that you were starting to feel a little stale? But you said it was hard to walk away from a fantastic production team and the fat paychecks. So maybe this was a blessing in disguise."

Did Simone have a point? "Well . . . maybe. But I always meant to write my own ending, you know? I was going to walk away from the show when *I* was ready. I don't like it when other people write my endings for me."

"The way Chris did?"

She winced. "That's different. I wasn't planning to walk away from Chris."

"Maybe you should have."

Kate stared at her. "What are you talking about?"

Simone hesitated. "It wasn't my place to say so, but . . . I was never sure that Chris was the right guy for you. I mean, I know the two of you got along great. You made a good team in a lot of ways. But you never seemed really passionate about each other."

Kate looked away. "I don't know if I'm the passionate type. In my writing, yes. But I don't think I'm cut out for it in real life. I mean, look at that night at the club. I went out looking for excitement, and nothing happened. And upon sober reflection, I think that was for the best."

"Whoa. You don't think Ian qualifies as exciting?"

"Nothing's going to happen with Ian."

"It could if you wanted it to."

Kate shook her head. "I couldn't handle a guy like that. You know the women at the network have the lowdown on every bachelor there, right?"

"Sure."

"Ian never goes out with anyone he works with, which is a point in his favor—but the word on the street is that he's hooked up with a wide selection of Manhattan women. And he's never with any of them for more than a few weeks. This is not a guy who does relationships."

"So don't have a relationship with him. Have the rebound fling of a lifetime."

"I don't think I'm cut out for a fling."

"I thought you wanted to shake up your life a little."

"Well, I've reconsidered. I wouldn't know what to do with a man like Ian. Why do you think I was with Chris? He was sweet and gentle and—"

"A cheating bastard."

"Okay, yes, the cheating thing took me by surprise. But even though I might fantasize about Ian—"

"I *knew* it!"

"There's a big difference between fantasy and reality. I think I'm better off sticking to the slow lane when it comes to romance. I know it didn't work out with Chris, but I still think a man like him would be more my speed."

Simone opened her mouth, but Kate held up a hand. "That's enough about my love life. You're the one who called *me*, remember? Tell me about this director. What's his name?"

Simone sighed. "Zachary Hammond."

"That sounds familiar."

Simone slumped back against the wall. "Seven years ago he played Orlando in the movie version of *As You Like It*."

Kate snapped her fingers. "Of course! That's the one you made me see with you twice. And then, as I recall, you saw it by yourself another three times."

"I was interested in the costume design," Simone said stiffly.

"Of course you were."

Simone slumped lower. "Okay, fine. I was totally obsessed with Zach Hammond that summer. It broke my heart when he announced that he was leaving the movies to focus on theater directing."

"And now he comes to New York to work with your company. A very Shakespearean twist of fate, wouldn't you say?"

"I would not. Especially since he's making me get on a plane." She sat up straight and smacked herself on the forehead. "I forgot to tell you worst part. Zach was outside the theater when Jessica dropped me off last night, and she recognized him. She hopped out of the car and introduced herself and talked for ten minutes about how she'd seen him perform *Hamlet* in London and how much she loved all his movies, blah blah blah . . . and then she asked him to do a reading from Shakespeare at her wedding."

Kate's jaw dropped. "What did he say?"

"He said yes."

"He *did*?"

"Well, she sort of cornered him. She asked what the performance schedule was for the play and found out that opening night isn't until two weeks after the wedding. Then she talked about what great friends we are and how I'm one of her bridesmaids—as if knowing *me* was going to be some kind of in with Zach Hammond—and then she hit him with it."

"You must have been mortified."

"I wanted to die. Once she finally left, I apologized and told him he didn't have to do it. He just laughed and said he didn't mind at all."

"Wow. Handsome as sin and a nice guy to boot."

"I don't think he agreed because he's nice. I think the whole situation amused him."

Kate thought for a moment. "Okay, so what brought on the code red? The prospect of taking a six-hour flight across the Atlantic, your hopeless crush on a former movie star, or the fact that Jessica is making him perform at the wedding from hell?"

Simone slumped down again, sliding her hands into the pockets of her jeans. "I don't know. Probably all three. I need chocolate."

"Do you want to go to Jacques Torres?"

"God, yes."

∽

On Tuesday afternoon, Kate met Jacob after school again. It was raining, so they took a cab back to Ian's apartment. They bought hot chocolates at the Starbucks next door and carried them upstairs to watch *The Avengers* on Ian's big-screen TV.

Once the movie was over, Jacob disappeared to do his homework and Kate pulled out her tablet to work on a pitch for an appointment the following week. But the project she'd decided to present turned out to be uninspiring, and after half an hour she put the tablet back in her purse and got up to get a glass of water.

She'd learned over time that when she felt blocked creatively, it helped to take a break and let her subconscious work out the problem. After she drank her water, she wandered around Ian's living room for a few minutes, wondering why it was so devoid of personality. There was very little of Ian—or Jacob—to be seen here. Everything she saw was high-quality, expensive, and generic.

There was more of Jacob in his room, of course. Maybe Ian's bedroom revealed something about the man who slept there, too. And there were other rooms she hadn't been in. Maybe he had an office or a study that was full of personal photos and knickknacks.

Not that she would ever know. She had no reason, absolutely none, to go snooping through Ian's apartment.

Of course, the more she thought about it, the more she wanted to. What made Ian Hart tick? What did he love, hate, fear, wish for?

She remembered what Simone had said at the Met: that she was hanging onto the fact that Ian had cancelled her show as a way to avoid dealing with other feelings that might be developing.

There was no doubt that Ian was a complex man. He didn't do relationships, but he had a chivalrous side. He could be cold-blooded when it came to business, but it was obvious that he loved his nephew with all his heart. She'd spent the last two years thinking of him as a refugee from a Brooks Brothers catalog, but it turned out that underneath those conservative suits he was sporting tattoos—tattoos he never let anyone see.

Kate went to the beige leather sofa and sat down, pulling out her phone and staring at it for almost a minute. Then she pulled up Ian's contact info and started typing an email.

So when are you going to tell me about your tattoos? When you got them, where you got them, why you got them?

The moment she hit send, she regretted it. Ian was at work, for God's sake. She knew what he was like at work: all business.

She got up from the couch and started to pace. Not only had she bothered Ian with a trivial personal question in the middle of a workday, but now she was stuck waiting for a response that probably wouldn't come.

She felt like a high school girl who texted a guy and then had to spend the rest of the day waiting for him to text her back . . . if he ever did. What in the world had possessed her to—

Beep.

She went back to the sofa and sat down before opening the email. Her heart was beating absurdly fast.

I suppose I might be persuaded to tell you someday . . . for the right price.

She read it over several times, her heart still racing and warmth creeping into her cheeks. After a moment she realized she was grinning like an idiot.

Was he flirting? It sounded like he was flirting. But maybe he was just teasing. Teasing wasn't the same thing as flirting.

Not that she wanted him to flirt with her. Hadn't she made a huge point of explaining that they shouldn't cross that line?

But flirting wouldn't really cross the line, would it? Kissing would cross the line. There was a big difference between kissing and flirting.

If he even was flirting. The more she read his email, the less certain she felt.

What kind of price are we talking?

Send.

A simple question. Not overtly flirtatious but not closing the door, either.

What are you offering?

Oh, great—the ball was back in her court.

She chewed on her lip for a moment.

Do you have a sweet tooth? I'm a pretty good baker.

Definitely a less flirtatious tone. It was the safer course, but she couldn't help feeling a twinge of regret as she hit send.

That seems like a fair trade. We can discuss terms when I get home tonight.

He'd followed her lead in backing away from the flirting precipice—and, without being rude, had clearly indicated that they shouldn't do any more emailing while he was at work.

Well done, Ian.

Well done, both of them, really.

So there was no reason to feel disappointed as she put her phone away and went to the bookshelves to pick out something to read.

There was a fairly wide selection. The fiction choices ranged from spy novels and thrillers to Ernest Hemingway and William Faulkner, and the nonfiction included business books, military history, historical biographies, and sports biographies. All pretty typical stuff for a—

Kate froze. Tucked away on the bottom shelf and partly hidden by a floor lamp was something she recognized.

She moved the lamp out of the way and crouched down to look more closely.

It couldn't be—but it was.

An original Dungeons & Dragons set.

Her older brother had been a player, and he'd used this identical set. How well she remembered the Dungeon Master's Guide, not to mention the many-sided dice used to determine the events of the game, from character creation to battle outcomes.

This was one of the original bastions of geek culture. Could it be that cynical, practical, money-minded Ian Hart had once let his imagination roam in the world of swords and sorcery?

Of course, the set might not even belong to him. It could be Jacob's—although she doubted it. This was a vintage collectible. But a friend or relative of Ian's might have left it here. Or maybe it did belong to him but wasn't something he'd ever used much. Kate knew how relics of youth could follow people through the years for no particular reason.

Kate sat down cross-legged on the floor, lifted the lid from the box, and pulled out one of the well-worn manuals.

property of ian hart had been written on the inside front cover in large block letters.

A slow smile spread across her face.

There was additional evidence of usage throughout. A young Ian had scribbled notes in the margins, and there were several character sheets stuck in between the pages. The one he'd played most often was a human warrior he'd named Galahad.

Kate closed the book and ran her fingers over the cover.

She ought to put it all back. Even though she hadn't technically been snooping—the box was on a bookshelf in the living room, after all—she was quite sure that Ian would prefer to keep this part of his past private. The decent thing to do would be to replace the set where she'd found it.

A few minutes later, she'd carried the box over to the sofa and displayed the contents on the coffee table: rule books, dice, miniatures, and a faded map drawn on an enormous sheet of graph paper.

Then she curled up with a Robert Ludlum novel she'd taken from the bookshelf and waited for Ian to come home.

∼

Ian's pulse kicked up a notch as he rode the elevator to his apartment. Since Kate had emailed him earlier that day, he'd pulled his phone out several times to reread their exchange, a smile tugging at his mouth every time he did.

He'd come up with step two in his plot to woo her into his bed. He'd invite her to stay for dinner with him and Jacob, and at some point during the evening he'd casually mention that it might be fun to do something while Jacob was away that weekend with his grandparents.

He wasn't used to putting this much work into the planning stages of a seduction. For most of his adult life he'd relied on "Can I buy you a drink?" and "How about we get out of here?" to achieve a pretty impressive closing percentage.

Of course, living with Jacob had put a crimp in his social life. He had to either plan ahead for a babysitter—something he didn't like to do too often, since he spent so much time away from Jacob because of work—or limit his dates to the one weekend a month Jacob went to Philadelphia to see his grandparents.

The truth was, he hadn't really minded the change. He tended to avoid serious relationships, and casual dating had begun to pall even before Jacob had moved in with him. In the past year he'd been out only a handful of times.

But his attraction to Kate felt different. He was never sure what she would do or say next, and her determination to resist him brought out some primitive male instinct to conquer that felt like a shot of whiskey in his veins.

It had been a long time since he'd felt this alive around a woman.

Part of that feeling came from the times he'd gone to her rescue. Even though Spike wasn't real, Ian had found himself at home in his skin. There was something cathartic about being able to say exactly what he felt, not to mention showing his tattoos to the world.

He'd been an executive for almost ten years, but the truth was, wearing a $2,000 suit to a board meeting could feel more like playing a part than taking Kate home on a Harley did.

And it didn't feel nearly as good.

Bridezilla had had it all wrong when she'd told Kate that a man felt better standing next to a petite woman. Standing next to Kate—especially when there was that spark of challenge in her eyes—made him feel more vital and powerful and masculine than he ever had in his life.

As he turned the key in his lock, his anticipation rose, and he felt a surge of electricity the moment he saw Kate in the living room. She was curled up on the couch with a book, and when she met his eyes and smiled slowly, he felt it in his groin.

"Well, hello there," she purred, and for one heady moment he thought he might not need a seduction plan after all.

Then he saw the coffee table.

So much for feeling powerful and masculine. In a flash he was reduced to the gawky thirteen-year-old he'd once been, playing Dungeons & Dragons for hours with like-minded eighth-graders.

Doing his best to ignore Kate's grin, he dropped his briefcase on the floor and went to look over the display. Then he sat down in an armchair across from her.

"I might have known you'd find this stuff. Did you use some kind of geek radar?"

"It just goes to show you should never make assumptions about someone," Kate said. "In a million years I would never have guessed you had this in your past. And in case you were wondering, I didn't snoop. It was on a shelf right out in the open."

He shook his head. "I should have destroyed the evidence years ago."

Kate was still smiling at him, and he found himself smiling back. The sun had set, but Kate had turned on only a few lamps. She looked beautiful in the soft light, her skin impossibly smooth, her hair as bright and shiny as a copper penny. Her elbow was resting on the arm of the couch, and her cheek was pillowed on her hand, her head cocked to the side. She looked comfortable, her feet tucked under her in her favorite sitting position.

He liked seeing her look like that—like she belonged in his apartment.

He glanced down at the miniatures she'd arranged on the coffee table. So what if Kate knew he'd once played Dungeons & Dragons? Considering how proud she was of her own geekdom, this could actually work in his favor.

"I want to hear about your days as Galahad," she said. "And you were a Dungeon Master, too, weren't you?"

He leaned back in his chair and laced his fingers behind his head. "I thought you wanted to hear about my tattoos."

"I want to hear about that, too. Basically, I want the story of your life."

"Really."

"Yep."

He nodded thoughtfully, letting a beat go by while he pulled off his suit jacket and loosened his tie. "I tell you what. If you stay and have pizza with Jacob and me, I'll give you the story of my life afterwards. Some of it, anyway."

Kate raised her eyebrows. "You sure drive a hard bargain. In exchange for giving me what I want, you're going to force me to eat pizza? You must be brutal at the negotiation table. Are you going to make me have dessert, too?"

"Smart-ass. Is that a yes?"

"You've talked me into it."

If he had his way, this wouldn't be the only thing he talked Kate Meredith into.

∽

"I've still got homework to finish," Jacob said once they'd polished off two pizzas. "Is it okay if I take my Oreos into my room?"

"Sure," Ian said. After Jacob left he told Kate, "We can have our cookies out on the terrace, if you like."

"You have a *terrace*?"

Kate might not be susceptible to his usual moves, but it was a rare New Yorker who could fail to be impressed by an apartment with a balcony.

He grinned at her. "See? My soulless palace of luxury has a few advantages."

She rolled her eyes and followed him into his study, where French doors led out to a brick-walled terrace.

"Okay, it's nice," she acknowledged, looking around at the lush ivy, the potted shrubs, and the rosebushes in wooden planters. As she set her glass of milk on the wrought-iron table and took a seat on one of the cushioned chairs, Ian flipped a switch that turned on fairy lights entwined with the ivy.

"Okay, it's beautiful."

"Would you like a glass of wine?" he asked as he lit the votives in the center of the table.

She shook her head. "I think I'll stick with milk. It's the perfect pairing with Oreos."

"Very true."

As he sat down in the chair beside hers, she dipped a cookie into her milk and took a bite.

"The setting is perfect," she said after a moment. "A beautiful terrace, candlelight, and Oreos. The time has come for Scheherazade to tell a story."

"Am I Scheherazade in this scenario?"

"Yep."

"So that would make you the sultan."

She crossed her legs and waved a cookie in the air like a royal scepter. "I await my nightly entertainment."

He finished his last Oreo, cleared his throat dramatically, and began.

"Once upon a time, there was a young man who lived in Brooklyn with his mother and sister. When he was in eighth grade, he discovered Dungeons & Dragons."

Kate nodded. "That's when my brother got into the game, too."

"Did you ever play?"

"A little . . . but I got sucked into computer and video games pretty early. That's where I spent my time."

"I never got into those. It was just Dungeons & Dragons for me until high school."

"I still have a hard time visualizing that. D&D is hard-core geeky."

"You have to bear in mind that young Ian Hart was very different from the handsome, sexy, powerful man you see before you now."

Kate snorted.

"At thirteen, he was as nerdy as they come—tall and skinny, with braces and acne, and so wrapped up in his fantasy role-playing game, he could have been one of those cautionary tales about kids who lose their grip on reality."

"So what changed?"

"One day at recess, the school's basketball coach spotted him shooting hoops and recognized some latent talent for the game. Or it might have been the fact that Ian was tall and the JV team needed a center. Whatever the reason, the coach encouraged Ian to try out for the team, and he made it."

"A turning point in our plot."

"Not only was Ian good at sports, but he actually enjoyed them. This discovery coincided with the braces coming off his teeth, his skin clearing up, and his muscular development finally catching up with his height. In short, our hero suddenly had access to a coolness factor previously unattainable—just in time for his freshman year of high school, when his family left Brooklyn and moved to the Bronx."

"Did he turn his back on his nerdy past?"

"He was fourteen years old and dating his first girlfriend, so we would need a word stronger than *yes* to answer that question."

"That sounds like the happy ending to your story, but there's obviously more. When do the tattoos come in?"

Ian hesitated. It had been easier telling Kate about his youth than he would have guessed, but he'd had enough for one night.

"Didn't Scheherazade keep her head by drawing out her stories? She'd end on a cliffhanger so the sultan would allow her to live one more night."

Kate put her elbow on the table and rested her chin in her hand. "Hmm. So you're saying you're going to make me wait to hear the rest of the story? I have to admit, it's a good technique. I'm already wondering when I'll get to hear it."

That's when it came to him: the perfect plan to seduce Kate Meredith. It was a little unorthodox, but then, so was she.

"I have an idea about that," he said casually. "Jacob's going away this weekend to visit his grandparents in Philadelphia. How about I come to your place on Saturday? If you'll supply the milk, I'll bring the Oreos—and I could bring Dungeons & Dragons, too. It would be fun to flex my Dungeon Master muscles after so many years."

He could practically see the wheels turning in her head as she thought about it. Everything about his proposal sent friendship signals instead of date signals, which should make Kate feel comfortable.

It worked. "Okay, that sounds like fun. I'd love to play Dungeons & Dragons. Maybe it'll get my imagination going and I'll be able to come up with a project I actually want to pitch to someone."

He felt a twinge of guilt. "You've been having trouble finding a new gig?"

She shrugged. "Don't worry about me, Hart. I'll figure out something eventually. I always do. Of course, I wouldn't have to figure out something if it weren't for you," she added, but she smiled as she said it, and there was no sting in her words.

Maybe she'd forgiven him for cancelling her show. He hoped so. Not only because he still felt guilty about it, but also because his plan for Saturday night would be a lot easier to execute if she wasn't still harboring resentment towards him.

But even if she were, he'd find a way around it. He wasn't going to let anything stop him this time. He wanted Kate Meredith, and he was going to have her.

Even if he had to use Dungeons & Dragons to do it.

Chapter Seven

Jacob had a big smile for her when Kate picked him up after school on Friday.

"Hi, Kate!"

"Wow, you look happy. Are you excited to see your grandparents this weekend?"

He nodded. "I always have an awesome time with them."

He was quiet for a few moments while Kate was hailing a cab. Then, after they'd climbed into the back, he suddenly said, "They asked me if I wanted to live with them after Mom died."

Kate was startled, but she managed not to show it. This was the first time Jacob had mentioned his mother's death to her.

"That was nice of them," she said. "Did you think about doing it?"

Jacob turned his head away to look out his window, and for a minute she thought he might not answer. But then he turned back. "I did think about it, but . . . Mom wanted Ian to be my guardian. She said so in her will. I figured . . . I figured . . . if that's what she wanted, then that's what I should do."

Kate nodded. They rode in silence for another minute or two, and then she said, "You've been living with your uncle for almost a year now. How do you think it's going?"

Jacob shrugged. "Okay, I guess."

He didn't say anything else, and Kate didn't push it. By the time they got to Ian's apartment, they'd started talking about the new Spider-Man movie coming out that summer.

Jacob's grandparents were driving into the city to pick him up, and they'd left a message to say they'd be there around five o'clock. It turned out that Jacob hadn't packed yet, so Kate helped him fill a suitcase while he continued chattering about Peter Parker.

The suitcase was packed and ready to go when it occurred to Kate that Jacob should bring a jacket. He wouldn't want to wear it now, since the day was so warm, but you never knew when it would cool down. She grabbed one from his closet and opened up the suitcase again.

Lying on top of his clothes was something she hadn't seen Jacob put in there, something that looked like a—

Suddenly he was there beside her, closing the suitcase again and pulling it away.

"I think this is all set. I don't need anything else. It's too warm for a jacket. I don't—"

He stopped and bit his lip. After a moment, Kate sat down on his bed.

"Listen, Jacob, whatever you might be working on is none of my business. I'll forget I ever saw it, if that's what you want." She paused. "But I have to say, what I saw looked pretty amazing. I'd love to see more, but only if it's okay with you."

He looked torn. "Well . . . I guess I have to show it to somebody sometime, right? I mean, if I ever want to do anything with it. And you've made awesome TV shows, and I know you like comic books."

He chewed on his lip for a few more seconds, and then he opened the suitcase again. He pulled out the bound pages she'd seen and held them close to his chest.

"Okay, so, I've been working on this for a long time. Do you want me to tell you about it, or do you want to just look at it?"

"Why don't you tell me about it first?" she said gently.

"Okay. Well. You know how a lot of fairy tales have wishes in them? You know, wishing wells and genies' lamps and things like that?"

Kate nodded.

"Do you know the story about the monkey's paw?"

"Sure. That's the one where a couple uses the monkey's paw to ask for three wishes, but they end up having terrible consequences. Right?"

"Right. There are other stories like that, too, about how people don't really know what they're doing when they make wishes, and how things happen that they didn't mean to have happen. So . . . you know how people sometimes talk about what superpower they would want if they could pick one? Like flying or being able to turn invisible or have superstrength or whatever?"

She nodded again.

"Okay, so, here's my idea. There's this guy who can give you any superpower you want, for a price. But you can only pick one, and you can't ever change it, and he won't tell you the price until after you agree to the deal. So you might have to steal the Hope Diamond or something, and you won't know until you've already said yes."

Kate was impressed. "That's a really cool idea, Jacob."

He bounced a little on the bed, and she remembered his bouncing like that at the baseball game. "That's not even the cool part. The cool part is, the people who get the superpowers they've always wanted don't always like the way it turns out. Sometimes they do, but not always, because there are—"

"Unintended consequences?"

He nodded vigorously. "Exactly. So . . . do you want to see it?"

"Of course!"

She took the book from Jacob, settled back against the headboard, and started to read.

She would have found something nice to say even if it had been the worst thing she'd ever seen, but it was wonderful. The drawing was rough, but Jacob had a real instinct for line and form, and there was an energy to the panels that made up for their lack of polish. She almost forgot he was there, waiting with bated breath for her verdict, as she turned the pages and met the five main characters whose lives would change by the end of the story.

"Oh, Jacob. It's fantastic."

He flushed up to the roots of his hair. "Really? You're not just saying that?"

"Absolutely not." She closed the book and handed it back to him. "This is incredible. In fact . . ."

And just like that, inspiration struck. She actually felt goose bumps on her arms.

"In fact, I have a proposal for you."

"What is it?"

"You don't have to answer right now. But I've got an appointment at a network next week, and I haven't decided what to pitch yet. The development executive I'm meeting with is known for taking risks with quirky, original projects. I want to pitch him your idea."

His eyes were huge behind his glasses. "You mean . . . you think it could be a TV show?"

"Yes—or a movie or miniseries. I should warn you, though, that networks say no to most of the projects they look at. And if they do pick it up, you should also know that you'd be giving up creative control. They'd have the rights to develop the story in whatever way they choose."

"Would you be a part of it, though? Like, as a writer or director or whatever?"

"Yes, if we get that far. But we probably won't. Even if they like the initial pitch, the project would still have to make it all the way up the chain of production approvals. In other words, Jacob, don't get your hopes up."

"It's totally too late for that," he said, and she laughed.

"Okay, I guess that's too much to expect. But even though you're excited now, I want you to think about it for a few days. There are a lot of things to consider. You might decide that TV is too commercial for you, and that you'd rather keep your idea as a graphic novel. You could submit it to a publisher or even self-publish it when you decide it's ready. I could help you do that."

He was bouncing on the bed again. "I'll think about it, but I already know my answer. I want you to pitch it at your appointment. Can we talk more about it when I get back?"

"Of course. That'll give you time to talk to Ian, too."

He stopped bouncing. "About that," he said, his tone more subdued.

"What?"

"I don't want to tell Ian. Not yet, anyway. When I first moved here, I used to work on my book out in the living room, and he'd say I should be outside in the fresh air, instead of cooped up inside, drawing. So then I started working on it in my room, so I could say I was doing homework if he knocked on the door." He paused. "It's just . . . I know he thinks comic books are stupid and he wishes I'd spend more time doing sports or whatever. So I don't want to say anything to him unless this actually turns into something. You know?"

She knew, all right. Jacob was afraid his uncle wouldn't take him or his work seriously. It was hard to show a creative project to the world—and sometimes it was easier to show total strangers than your own family.

On the other hand, she didn't feel comfortable keeping anything about Jacob from his uncle.

Still, what she'd told Jacob was true—only a small percentage of projects pitched to networks ever got picked up. Chances were, nothing would come of this anyway. "I guess we don't have to tell him right now. But if this actually ends up going somewhere, your uncle will have to be involved."

"All right. Thanks."

They heard the intercom buzz in the living room, and Jacob sprang to his feet. "They're here! Will you come down with me and meet them?"

"Sure. It's time for me to head home anyway."

She carried his suitcase down and shook hands with Jacob's grandparents, who seemed very nice—and were obviously crazy about their grandson.

She walked home, taking it slowly and thinking about Jacob's story. One of his main characters was a teenage boy who'd lost both his parents. The parallels were obvious and made her think of the stories she'd written over the years that echoed her own dreams and fears and subconscious hauntings.

She remembered telling a fan at a convention that people have been telling stories for as long as language has existed, and that stories are one of the most powerful tools we have for navigating the pain and joy of being alive.

Apparently Jacob had already figured that out. Pretty impressive for an eleven-year-old. Of course, he was a pretty impressive kid in general.

And his uncle, she was starting to think, wasn't too bad himself.

∼

The next day, Kate woke up feeling like a kid on the first day of summer vacation. At first there was just a vague sensation of happiness without a particular cause, but when she rolled onto her side to pet Gallifrey, memory returned.

Ian was coming over tonight.

Not for a date, of course. For a game of Dungeons & Dragons, of all things. It didn't get much more un-date-like than that.

So there was no reason for her to spend two hours that day cleaning her apartment, which was already pretty clean. But as she ran a dust cloth over her furniture, relishing the smooth patina of the different woods and the faint lemon scent of the cleaner she used, she found herself smiling like a teenage girl on the day of her prom.

She felt less like a teenager and more like a woman when she changed her sheets. It was impossible not to imagine Ian lying there, his big body dominating her queen-size bed.

Of course, she'd never see him here in real life. A game of Dungeons & Dragons was the least likely scenario for foreplay ever, which was probably why Ian had chosen that particular activity. She'd made such a point of clarifying the boundaries between them there was no chance he'd try to cross the line.

As she acknowledged that fact to herself, she straightened her blue silk comforter over the clean white sheets and smoothed out the wrinkles.

The silk felt good under her hands, like most of the things in her apartment. She always paid attention to texture when she was decorating, choosing to fill her home with things she enjoyed touching.

Thoughts of touching led inevitably to thoughts of Ian. Ian dancing with her . . . Ian driving her home on a motorcycle . . . Ian pushing her back against the wall and kissing her like some kind of barbarian conqueror.

All at once she gave in to fantasy. She threw herself onto the bed and rolled onto her back, closing her eyes and imagining Ian on top of her, pressing her into the mattress.

God, that big body. Chris was a couple of inches shorter than she was, and though that fact had never bothered her, she suspected it had bothered him. The few times she'd put on high heels for a special occasion, he'd always suggested she change into flats—so she'd be more comfortable.

But Ian was taller than she even when she wore four-inch spikes. It might not be politically correct to relish his physical dominance, but the truth was, when she remembered how easily he'd pushed her against the wall and how the breadth of his shoulders had blocked everything else from her view, she felt like a Victorian maiden in need of lavender water and a fainting couch.

Of course, fantasy was one thing and reality another. The list of cons for letting anything happen with Ian was pretty long.

Maybe Simone was right about her clinging to this one a little too hard, but the fact was, he had cancelled her show.

The two of them were polar opposites in a lot of ways, with different priorities, talents, interests, and values.

He was a Yankees fan.

She'd just broken up with her fiancé and needed time to recover from that before she even thought about getting involved with someone new.

When she *was* ready to go out again, Ian was the last man in the world she should consider dating. This was because:

He was not a guy who did relationships. It was widely known that when Ian hooked up, it was just that—a hookup. His liaisons rarely lasted more than a few weeks.

Ian's aversion to relationships occasionally made the jump from her con list to her pro list. As Simone said, every woman was entitled to a hot rebound fling once in her life. And what better candidate for that kind of relationship than Ian Hart?

But every time she considered that point, she always ended up putting the item back on her con list. The truth was, despite her aborted quest for rebound sex that night at the club, she knew in her heart that one-night stands were not her thing.

Another item on the con list: she was actually starting to think that she and Ian could be friends. Letting something happen between them would only screw that up.

There was Jacob to consider, too. Muddying things between her and Ian couldn't possibly be good for his nephew.

Her pro list, on the other hand, consisted of only one item.

Ian was the sexiest man she'd ever known, and the chemistry she felt when she was with him was like nothing she'd ever experienced.

Funny how sometimes that one item seemed to outweigh everything on her con list.

But the part of her that wanted to jump Ian's bones was the crazy part, and not to be encouraged.

Simone employed several strategies when she didn't want to sleep with a guy but needed help to bolster her willpower. Her favorite was the wear-hideous-underwear strategy—the idea being that a woman in granny panties will never risk their being seen.

Kate decided to go with a different approach. Thinking about Ian made her feel sexy, and even though she wasn't going to act on it, she enjoyed the feeling so much that she didn't want to ruin it by wearing ratty underwear.

So instead she put on her best lingerie. The effect would be the same, since if Ian ever saw what she was wearing under her clothes, he'd conclude that she'd been expecting him to disrobe her at some point during the evening, which would be even more humiliating than letting him see her in granny panties.

So she put on the birthday present she'd gotten this year from Simone. It had been something of a gag gift, since Kate wasn't the sexy-lingerie type, but she secretly adored the black lace set. It fit exquisitely, and the bra and panties were so delicate and impractical that Kate had always thought of them as objects to look at, rather than wear. She'd never even taken the tags off... until now.

Ian was coming over at eight with Oreos, milk, and Dungeons & Dragons. A very unromantic setup, which was definitely for the best—but that didn't mean she couldn't indulge herself beforehand. Ian didn't need to know that she took a jasmine-scented bubble bath before putting on gossamer-fine lingerie—especially since it was hidden under jeans and a tee shirt.

But she would know . . . and she'd enjoy the secret.

Ever since that night at the club, she'd been taking more pleasure in her physicality: standing up straighter, wearing her hair down every so often, even making an appointment for a leg wax the week before. Part of it was undoubtedly a reaction to her breakup with Chris, but it was also the realization that a man like Ian Hart could be attracted to her.

One dance and one kiss had done wonders for her self-esteem.

By the time Andreas sent him up that night, she was confident that she'd gotten her fantasies out of her system and was ready to enjoy a relaxed, platonic evening.

Then she opened the door.

Ian stood there in faded jeans and a black button-down shirt, looking sexy and powerful and good enough to eat. There was stubble on his jaw and a half smile on his face, and Kate wondered if it was possible for any woman to be friends with this man. She could see being his colleague or his enemy or his sex toy, but his friend?

Then he held up the Dungeons & Dragons box and a bag of Oreos, and her heart rate slowed a little. A man who'd once played a fantasy adventure game had more layers to his personality than were immediately apparent. He might even be friend material after all.

"Ready for milk and cookies and sword fighting?" he asked.

She stood back to let him in. "Absolutely. Although I also have wine or beer if you want something stronger."

She'd been on the fence about suggesting alcohol, but a glass of wine would help her relax—and it was Saturday night, after all.

But as soon as the words were out of her mouth, she worried that Ian would misinterpret her intentions. Maybe he'd think she was trying to get him drunk so she could take advantage of him.

"Sure, wine sounds great."

He spoke casually, so she figured it was okay.

"You can set up the game on the coffee table," she said as she headed for the kitchen. "Do you prefer red or white?"

"Red."

Her grandparents had been wine connoisseurs, and she'd been working her way through their collection over the last few years. She hesitated a moment, wondering what to choose, then decided on a Château Lafite Rothschild. She filled two glasses but left the bottle in the kitchen, not wanting to be accused of wine snobbery. If Ian knew anything about the subject, he'd know this particular vintage would fetch well over $3,000 at auction.

Ian was sitting on the living room floor with his back against the sofa. There was a collection of multicolored polyhedral dice on the coffee table, along with a handful of miniatures and several sheets of paper.

She set the wineglasses down before sitting on the floor on the other side of the table. When he lifted his glass, she lifted hers, too.

"To friendship," he said, and she felt a rush of relief—and a twinge of disappointment she immediately repressed.

"To friendship," she echoed, and they both drank.

Ian's eyes widened. "Holy hell," he said, staring at the glass in his hand before taking another sip. "You have a whole bottle of this?"

She nodded. "My grandparents loved wine, and they left me their collection."

"Damn," he said appreciatively, inhaling the aroma. "I didn't realize you knew anything about wine. I never saw you drink at a network party."

"I don't like to drink at work, even if it's a social event. It's too easy to have one too many and say something stupid."

"You like to stay in control," he said thoughtfully.

"Well, sure. At work, anyway. Doesn't everyone?"

"Probably," he agreed, taking one more sip, then setting his glass down. "Are you ready to get started?"

She nodded. "I played a little in high school, but I don't remember much. I know you use the dice to create your character, though."

"You can—but sometimes a Dungeon Master rolls characters in advance for a particular adventure." He slid one of the sheets of paper over to her. "I created one for you, but if you don't like her, we can roll one from scratch."

Character Name: Red Sonja
Race: Human
Class: Fighter

There were several other details listed, including the armor she wore and the weapons she fought with.

Kate looked up from the sheet with a grin. "You're letting me be Red Sonja? I'm surprised you even know who she is."

"I didn't before that night at the club when Arthur announced that you were a dead ringer for her." He nodded towards the framed print on the wall. "I have to admit, I can see the resemblance."

"Thank you, kind sir. And I'd love to play this character. Role-playing games are all about wish fulfillment, right? And I always wanted to be a warrior."

"You've never been a warrior in real life?"

"I assume you mean metaphorically, and no. I create stories about heroes and heroines who fight evil, but in my own life I've never been very brave."

Ian started to speak but then stopped himself. Kate wondered what he'd been about to say. She almost asked him, but then Gallifrey jumped up on the coffee table and swatted at one of the dice.

Ian picked it up from the floor as Gallifrey knocked another one off the table, and Kate scrambled to her feet.

"He's looking for dinner," she explained, and went to the kitchen to feed him.

"Explain to me why people like cats so much?" Ian asked when she came back.

She sat on the floor again, cross-legged this time. "Do you know what Jean Cocteau said about cats?"

"No, but I bet you're about to change that."

"He said, 'I love cats because I love my home, and after a while they become its visible soul.'"

"That's a little metaphysical for me."

"But it's true. For me, the soul of a home should be comfort—and cats are the very essence of comfort. When I see Gallifrey curled up on my bed in a patch of sunlight, it makes me feel warm and cozy and happy. And that's how I want my home to feel."

He looked around her living room for a moment, his eyes moving over the furniture, the art on her walls, the books and knickknacks on her shelves.

"You've succeeded. I don't think I've ever been in a place that feels warmer and cozier than this one."

She was pleased by the compliment. "Well, thanks. That's nice of you to say."

Then she remembered the comment she'd made about his apartment. When she glanced at his face, she knew he was remembering it, too.

"A soulless palace of luxury," he murmured.

She cleared her throat. "Yes, well . . . that wasn't a very nice thing to say. I'm sorry about that."

"Don't be. It's true. I hired a decorator and told her to make it look professional—which she did."

"Your terrace feels different. There's definitely some soul out there."

"Thanks, but I can't take credit for that, either. I just kept it the way it was when I moved in." He cocked his head to the side. "Speaking of soul—didn't you describe me to Simone as an evil bastard without one?"

This time she refused to be embarrassed. "Indeed I did. Didn't you once describe me to the VP of sales as a flaky artist with zero grasp on reality?"

A corner of Ian's mouth twitched. "I may have said something like that."

She picked up her wineglass and held it towards him. "Truce?"

He clinked his glass against hers. "Truce."

They started the game soon afterwards, and it didn't take long for Kate to get into it. She'd played Dungeons & Dragons only a few times, but she'd been an RPG aficionado for years, and the language and conventions of the world were easy to pick up.

Her quest was to rescue a handsome prince from the ruined castle where he was being held captive.

"I thought you'd appreciate the role reversal," Ian told her.

"How very gender-neutral of you."

She was surprised at how easily he got into it, too. Ian obviously enjoyed his role as Dungeon Master, using the pseudomedieval terminology of the fantasy world with ease and seeming to take a lot of pleasure in unleashing mayhem on her character.

Before she could enter the castle, she had to fight her way past a few dozen monsters and steal a key from a troll's lair. Once she conquered those challenges, she stood at the door that led down to the dungeon where the prince was imprisoned.

"I try to open the door."

"It's locked."

"I use the key I stole from the troll."

Ian rolled one of the dice he used to determine outcomes. "The key works, and the door opens. You find yourself in a small antechamber. It's pitch black."

"I light my lantern."

"You're already carrying your sword and shield," he reminded her.

"Right. Okay, I sling my shield over my shoulder but keep my sword out. I use my free hand to hold the lantern."

"Once the lantern is lit, you see that you're not alone. Coming towards you across the chamber is a human warrior holding a broadsword. He stops when he sees you. 'Who are you, fair maiden? What has brought you to this place?'"

"I don't sheathe my sword, but I don't attack yet." She let her voice deepen a little to indicate she was now speaking for her character. "I am Red Sonja, a warrior who has come here on business of my own. Who are you?"

"I am Galahad."

Kate shot a glance at him, but his expression was the neutral one she'd mentally dubbed his Dungeon Master poker face.

"Galahad," she repeated cautiously. "The name is not unknown to me. I believe you are a warrior of some renown, one who is allied with the forces of good. What quest has brought you here?"

"I am here because of the words of a seer. She told me that if I came to this place I should look upon the fairest lady in all the land, and I had a great desire to do so. And I have not been disappointed."

Kate dropped her eyes to her character sheet. She held one of the dice in her hand, and now she squeezed it into her palm.

Maybe if she hadn't had two glasses of wine, she would have maneuvered the game back on track, leaving Galahad behind. But a rare vintage was buzzing through her veins, and she couldn't stop herself from taking a cautious step into the unknown.

"Fair words are not always matched by noble actions. I am here to rescue a prince from this dark dungeon. Will you aid me on my quest?"

"How did you learn that a prince was imprisoned here?"

"In the kingdom of Anduria I met the king's wise woman. It was she who bade me seek the king's son in this place."

"Did this wise woman wear a moonstone around her neck?"

Her eyes flicked up to his for an instant. "She did."

"Then your wise woman and my seer are one and the same. There is no prince in these dungeons, my lady. There is only the man you see before you."

A thousand things prickled her skin—adrenaline, excitement, fear, uncertainty.

She couldn't meet his eyes again. She stared down at her hands and saw they were both clenched into fists.

She tried to draw air into her lungs, but she couldn't seem to manage it. Her heart was pounding wildly.

What should she do? What should she say?

Then she heard Ian's voice again. "Galahad throws down his sword and shield and approaches you. 'My lady, when I look at you I am consumed by desire. If you will lay down your arms for this one night, I will bring you such pleasure as you have never known.'"

Her cheeks burned. "You seem very sure of your abilities in this area."

"I am," he said, his voice low and seductive. "I'll be the best you ever had. If you let me be your rebound, Kate, I swear you won't regret it."

When she finally met his eyes, she couldn't look away.

"Kate," he said softly.

A shiver went through her. By using her name, he was taking them from fantasy to reality.

"Kate," he said again.

Her heart was pounding. "Yes?"

"Come here."

Chapter Eight

She wanted to. Oh, God, she wanted to. She'd never felt like this before—so terrified and so excited at the same time. Looking at Ian, seeing the coiled tension in his body and the naked hunger in his eyes, she felt a desire so deep and powerful it was like an ache in her very bones.

Her list of cons hadn't changed. There were still a lot of reasons not to do this.

But as she rose to her feet and walked around the coffee table, she decided she didn't give a damn about any of that. All she knew was that she wanted this man, and tonight she was going to have him.

The heat in his eyes seared her where she stood. He rose to his feet, too, looming over her for a moment before he sat down again, on the sofa this time, instead of the floor.

He looked like a sultan surveying a new harem girl, and suddenly her uncertainty was stronger than her desire. What if she was in over her head?

Ian had a lot more partners in his past than she had in hers. The promise in his eyes spoke of a breadth of sexual experience she didn't share.

She was positive that Ian was a man with skills. Moves. All-around carnal knowledge.

She, on the other hand, had no skills to speak of. She'd had vanilla sex with three different lovers. It had been pleasant enough, and she'd enjoyed it, but it would take more than the missionary position to satisfy Ian Hart.

Was he expecting her to be exciting and adventurous?

Maybe he expected her to do something right now. Something sultry.

She swallowed. "I don't know . . . I'm not sure what I . . . What happens now?"

One corner of his mouth lifted in a smile. "Now you take off your clothes."

Her face crimsoned over and her nipples hardened.

She crossed her arms over her chest to hide it. "Okay, a couple things," she said.

His mouth twitched. "A couple things?"

She cleared her throat. "First of all, you should know I'm wearing sexy underwear." His eyebrows lifted and she hurried on. "I wore them so I wouldn't be tempted to . . . to . . . do anything with you tonight. Because if you saw my sexy underwear you'd think I wanted this or planned it or expected it or—"

He shook his head. "I don't think that. I know you didn't expect this, Kate. I didn't expect it either. But I wanted it, and I'll do whatever it takes to make it happen."

Oh, God.

The red in her cheeks deepened. "The other thing is . . . I'm not really a make-out-in-the-living-room kind of girl. Or a make-out-with-the-lights-on kind of girl. So maybe we could, you know . . . move into the bedroom."

"Where we'll turn the lights off."

"If you don't mind."

His eyes gleamed. "There's something you need to remember."

"What?"

"I'm the Dungeon Master tonight—not you. My game, my rules. Got it?"

Her mouth opened, but nothing came out. Goose bumps swept over every inch of her skin.

It wasn't too late to say no. She could still turn tail and run. She could still—

"Okay," she whispered.

He shut his eyes for a second, and she wondered if he'd expected her to say no.

He opened them again. "I want to see your sexy underwear," he said, his voice husky.

"With the lights on and everything?"

"Yeah. And, Kate?"

"Yes?"

"Stop talking."

She opened her mouth, blinked, and closed it again. Then she took her courage in both hands, along with the hem of her tee shirt, and pulled it off over her head.

"Jesus," Ian breathed, and the look in his eyes as he stared at her breasts made her feel warm all over. She hesitated only a moment before she unzipped her jeans, slid them down her legs, and stepped out of them.

She saw Ian's hands twitch, and the muscles in his throat jumped as he swallowed.

"Come here," he grated out.

A rush of confidence made her shake her head. "I want to see your tattoos first. All of them."

His eyebrows went up. Then he leaned back against the sofa and stretched his arms out along the back, opening his legs in a *V*.

"I'm all yours," he said.

She stepped into the space he'd made for her and leaned over him to undo his top button. She didn't meet his eyes, but she felt his gaze on her, hot and hungry.

As she moved to the next button, she glanced farther down his body and felt a sudden flash of lust when she saw the erection pushing against his jeans.

He wanted her.

He wanted *her*.

The thrill of that knowledge made her slow down as she moved to his third button, letting her hair fall forward to brush against the bare skin she was exposing.

"Vixen," he whispered, and her lips curved up in a smile.

When she undid the last button, his shirt fell open.

Sweet mother of God.

She'd never seen a male torso like this outside of the movies. Broad, powerful, and with a ridged abdomen that drew the eye even farther downward, towards what was still hidden under blue denim.

There was only one tattoo on his chest. It was a phoenix done in black, the effect like a pen-and-ink illustration.

She gave in to the urge to touch him, letting her fingers trace over the tattoo. His stomach muscles tensed as he sucked in a breath.

"It's beautiful," she said softly, her gaze lifting to meet his.

"Kate," he whispered. "My God, Kate."

She went still. There was heat and need and passion in his eyes, but also something new. Something she hadn't seen before.

"Kiss me," he said, his voice rough and demanding but also beseeching.

Letting herself fall against him was a relief so intense, it was like the cessation of pain. Her breasts pressed against his chest as she slid her arms around his neck, and in the next instant her mouth was on his.

He groaned, and she felt the vibration in her bones. His tongue slid into her mouth and his hands went everywhere, sliding into her hair, roaming down her back, gripping her hips.

When she realized she was rubbing herself against his erection like a cat in heat, she should have been embarrassed. But the fire inside her left no room for anything but need, and instead of pulling away she reached down between their bodies and fumbled for the zipper of his jeans.

He broke the kiss and grabbed her upper arms.

"Wait," he panted.

"Wait?" she repeated incredulously. The heat and throbbing between her legs was unbearable, and the need to have Ian inside her was not going to be denied.

His hold on her arms tightened, and with a powerful twist he flipped them over so she was on her back beneath him.

The sudden move sent sofa cushions scattering, and Kate sucked in a breath as she stared up into Ian's face. His eyes were fierce, and the weight of his body on hers was so deliciously perfect that she moaned.

"Why did you say 'wait'?" she asked. "I don't want to wait."

"There are things I want to do to you before my jeans come off."

And then he was kissing his way down her body, his mouth closing over one breast through the lace of her bra. He covered the other with his hand while she pushed herself into him almost frantically, the sensations he was creating pooling like lava between her legs.

He kissed lower, dipping his tongue into her naval and making her jump. He put his hands on her hips, and suddenly she realized where he was heading.

She gripped his hair. "Wait."

He looked up at her. "I thought you didn't want to wait."

"It's just . . . I don't do that. That thing you're about to do."

He smiled, but there was nothing reassuring about it. It was more like the smile the wolf gave Little Red Riding Hood.

"That's right, you don't." He paused. "I do."

He reached up to unhook her bra and slip it off her shoulders. Then his hands were on the waistband of her panties, and he slid them down and off.

She was naked. She was naked, and the lights were on, and Ian had settled between her legs like he was expecting to stay awhile.

"Ian—"

He grinned that wolfish grin again. "My game, my rules. Remember?"

"I—"

"Trust me, Kate. And stop talking."

He pressed his thumbs into her softest skin, spreading her open. Then his mouth was on her.

Oh, God.

It was so intense she couldn't stay still. She writhed against him, and when he gripped her hips she had a sudden wild wish that his hands would leave bruises on her body.

His hands were like iron, but his mouth was gentle. He licked her softly, thoroughly, and when his tongue flicked against her clitoris, she let out a cry before she could hold it back.

He did it again, and again.

If he kept doing that, she was going to come.

But then he pulled back and licked her again, his tongue delving deeper.

Oh God, oh God, oh God.

There was no more embarrassment or fear or shame. There was only the rising tide of her body and a pleasure so intense she was moaning, crying out, making sounds she'd never made in her life.

She was throbbing, quivering, aching for release. Just when she thought she couldn't stand it anymore, his tongue was *there*, and as she arched up to meet him he thrust two fingers inside her.

She came so hard it felt as if she'd left her body, transformed from flesh and blood into pure ecstasy.

"Ian!"

She heard his name as though someone else had called it out, and it sounded so good and so right, she said it again.

"Ian . . ."

When she came back into her body, she was trembling. Ian's hands had gone from iron-hard to whisper-soft, caressing her skin as he kissed his way back up her body.

Finally he rested his forehead against hers.

With a shock of surprise, she realized that he was trembling, too.

"Are you all right?" she whispered.

He laughed a little shakily. "Yeah, I'm all right. That was just . . . intense."

"For *you?*"

He pulled back and smiled down at her.

"Yeah, for me."

Then he kissed her, and the tang of her on his lips made her feel raw and wild and untamed.

"More," she said when he dragged his mouth from hers. "I want more."

He glanced at something over her shoulder. "I do, too. But I'm starting to like your idea of moving into the bedroom. For one thing, I wouldn't mind having a little more room to maneuver. And for another, your cat is staring at me."

Kate twisted her head to look, and there was Gallifrey, sitting on the arm of the sofa and gazing down at them.

"The bedroom it is," she agreed. "As long as we can keep the lights on," she added, and Ian gave her a quick, hard kiss before getting to his feet and pulling her up after him.

Her legs were shaky, so she hung onto his hand as they stumbled down the hall. And then they were in her bedroom and falling onto her silk comforter.

"I want these off now," Kate said, her hands going to his zipper, and this time he rolled onto his back and let her do what she wanted.

She tugged his jeans and boxers off, along with his socks. He'd dropped his shirt back in the living room, so now he was lying naked on her bed in all his glory.

And quite a bit of glory it was.

When she wrapped her hand around his erection, his whole body tensed.

"You're so big," she whispered, and he groaned.

Her hand tightened. "Do men really like to hear that?"

"Hell, yes. We're shallow that way."

"Then I should tell you that you're the biggest man I've ever been with. Of course, I've only been with three other guys, so it's not much of a sample group."

She began to move her hand up and down his length.

His breath hissed through his teeth. "Doesn't matter. Say it again."

She leaned close and whispered in his ear. "You're. So. *Big.*"

Her hand moved faster, and Ian groaned again.

She felt a rush of confidence. Deciding to go with it, she slid down the bed and took him in her mouth.

"*Jesus,*" he growled.

Whenever she'd gone down on Chris, he'd been gentle and considerate, letting her set the pace. It wasn't like that with Ian. He slid a hand into her hair and urged her to take him deeper, his voice and his touch hard and rough and demanding.

Her body responded with a flash of heat and rush of moisture at her center.

She wanted to make him come. She wanted it so much, she almost cried out in protest when he pulled away suddenly.

"That feels too good," he said, gasping for breath. "If you keep going I'll come, and I don't want to like that—not the first time. I want to be inside you."

His words made her shiver.

He rolled to the edge of the bed and grabbed his jeans from the floor, pulling a condom out of his back pocket.

Kate propped herself up on her elbows and watched him. "I see you came prepared."

His eyes were fierce and hot when he looked at her. "I told you I wanted this."

"I'm on the pill, if you—"

He shook his head. "I feel better using a condom."

"Okay."

For a moment they just stared at each other. Kate's body felt like a bowstring, taut and vibrating with anticipation. Ian's face was flushed, his jaw muscles tense and his neck muscles corded. He breathed as if he'd been running.

He kept his eyes on her as he ripped open the foil packet and rolled the condom over his shaft.

Then he did the last thing she expected.

He hesitated.

"You're sure you want this?" he asked, his voice low.

Her answer was immediate. "I've never wanted anything more in my life."

The words seemed to ignite something in him. His eyes darkened, and he pushed her back against the pillows. He used his knee to part her thighs, and then he was looming over her, his arms on either side of her shoulders, his biceps bunching.

His skin was hot, his muscles hard. For one instant he stayed like that, all coiled power and masculine intent. Then he found her center and pushed inside, just a few inches, and Kate arched her head back and cried out.

He froze. "You're tight," he said gruffly. "Am I hurting you?"

Was he insane? "Oh, God, Ian—I need more. Please, please . . ." She wrapped her legs around his waist and tried to urge him deeper.

He didn't need any more urging. He thrust inside her, the delicious friction sending shock waves through a thousand nerve endings. Again, and then again, while she made frantic, wordless cries and dug her nails into his shoulders. One more and he was all the way home, his ridged abdomen pressed against her belly and every inch of him buried inside her.

She'd never been invaded so thoroughly. The burn of it ignited into a deeper flame, a pleasure more decadent than anything she'd ever felt. All of her awareness was centered between her legs, at the place Ian had taken for his own.

"Open your eyes."

She hadn't realized she'd closed them.

Ian was gazing down at her like a barbarian king surveying a captive, his eyes dark and hooded.

"You're so beautiful," he whispered.

She slid her arms around his neck. "Kiss me."

He slanted his mouth onto hers, the slide of his tongue heart-poundingly erotic. Then he put his hands on her shoulders and rolled them over in one smooth motion.

Being on top had always made her feel self-conscious. But now she put her hands on Ian's chest and rode him with utter abandon, arching her back and gasping when he palmed her breasts.

Why hadn't she ever realized how incredible this position could be? With Ian's hard body below her, she felt like a goddess riding a thunderbolt.

So good. So good. If she shifted just a little, she'd—

Oh, God.

She'd never felt so sexy and powerful. She cried out as she came, waves of sensation making her body one fiery bolt of electricity.

Her skin was still tingling when Ian flipped them over again, and now it was his turn to take what he wanted.

He grabbed her wrists and pinned them above her head, and his thrusts inside her were deep and hard and almost savage.

The aftershocks of her own orgasm made her body clench around his, and she could feel how much that excited him. She wrapped her legs around his waist, and he sank inside with one last thrust, throbbing deep within her as he came.

His head dropped to her shoulder as he shuddered out his release.

When it was over he collapsed on top of her, his head still cradled against her shoulder. For a moment there was just their breathing, harsh and labored, and the wild pounding of their hearts. Then he rolled them onto their sides and gathered her close.

She could have stayed like that forever.

∼

Ian had never felt such a combination of sensations—ecstasy, excitement, comfort, peace. Pleasure pulsed through every nerve, and he couldn't stop his hands from moving over Kate's body, even though he could tell by her breathing that she was starting to fall asleep.

How could she sleep after that? Of course, he was usually out like a light five minutes after he came, but this had been so goddamn intense . . .

A delicate snore escaped her, and a rush of affection made him tighten his hold. God, she was adorable.

Ian had enjoyed sex since he'd first experienced it at the age of sixteen. He always had a good time in bed, and he did his best to make sure his partner had a good time, too.

But he'd decided a long time ago that the idea of soul-melding, heart-wrenching, mind-altering sex was just a fantasy. Sex felt great physically, and with a woman you liked it felt good emotionally, too. At its best, sex was fun and exciting and satisfying.

But this had been more.

As much as he'd wanted her, he'd never imagined it would be like that between them. Sweet, naive, inhibited Kate Meredith had been like fire, like lightning, like every fantasy he'd never thought could be true.

And she was so damn beautiful. He'd thought about her hair so much in the last few weeks that it was a relief, now, to run his hands through it. When she'd gone down on him, the sight of that copper silk against his hips and thighs and abdomen had driven him crazy.

He could never get tired of watching her. But, as impossible as it had seemed at first, the desire for sleep finally stole over him.

He smoothed a palm over Kate's curves one more time and pressed a kiss to her forehead. Then he closed his eyes and let himself drift.

∽

He must have rolled over at some point, because when he woke up he was on his stomach and Kate's hands were on his back.

He smiled into the pillow. "Hey," he said, his voice rusty with sleep.

Her hands stilled for a moment before they started to move again.

"Hey, yourself," she said softly. "I didn't get a good look at this tattoo before. It's beautiful."

She meant the hawk that stretched across his back, its outstretched wings touching the tips of his shoulder blades.

"Thanks," he said, his voice still muffled by the pillow. He could have rolled over, but her touch felt so good he didn't want her to stop.

"So . . . can I hear the rest of the story now?" she asked.

"The rest of the story?"

"Yes. You only told me the first part that night on your terrace. Remember? You said I could hear part two some other time."

Part two of his life history wasn't anything he liked to talk about. But he had sort of promised, and there was something about the intimacy of being here with Kate—the soft quiet of the room, the lateness of the hour, the feel of her fingertips tracing over his skin—that made it seem almost natural to tell her things he never told anyone.

He rolled onto his side and rested his head on his bent arm. Kate lay down beside him and mirrored his position, smiling into his eyes.

He'd forgotten how beautiful hers were. He reached out a hand to stroke her hair, then brushed the back of his knuckles over her cheek.

"You're sure you want to hear this?"

"Of course."

"Okay, then. Well." He thought about how to begin. "Right before I started high school, my mother was laid off. It had been hard to make ends meet even before that, and we had to leave our apartment in Brooklyn and move to a cheaper place in the Bronx. Mom started working two jobs, a call center during the day and waitressing at night."

"I take it your father was out of the picture."

"Yeah. He left when I was two, just after Tina was born. I don't remember him, and Mom never talked about him. We didn't have any other family, so it was just the three of us, and with my mom gone so much, it was my job to take care of my sister. We were living in a much rougher neighborhood than we'd grown up in, and I wanted to be sure I could protect her—not to mention myself. I'd gotten a lot bigger the year before, and I was a good athlete, which helped . . . but I also got in with a tough group of kids."

"A gang?"

"No, but we got into plenty of trouble. Alcohol and fighting, mostly."

"Is that when you got the tattoos?"

"Yeah."

"They really are beautiful," she said. "And they're sort of Dungeons & Dragons–y, aren't they? The swords and the hawk and the mythical creatures, and all the Celtic knot work."

"Celtic tattoos were hot at the time, but yeah, it probably also reminded me of my Dungeons & Dragons days. And since the point of getting inked up was to make people think I was tough, it's probably no accident that I chose warrior images."

She reached out and touched the phoenix on his chest. "If I were a guy with tattoos this gorgeous, I'd walk around shirtless from May to October."

That made him smile. "Not if you were a well-respected media executive."

"Well, maybe not. But that reminds me—I'm still missing a piece of your story. How did you go from tattooed troublemaker to well-respected media executive?"

He picked up his narrative again.

"The kids I hung out with got into trouble, like I said—but we usually managed to stay on the right side of the law. Then I fell in love with my best friend's older sister."

"How old was she?"

"Nineteen. I was seventeen, so I didn't think I had a chance. But she agreed to go out with me, and we started dating." He paused. "What I didn't realize was that she was using me as cover with her parents, who thought I was a nice boy in spite of my best efforts to be a badass. And compared with the guy she was actually dating, I *was* a nice boy."

"She was dating somebody else?"

"Yeah. A drug dealer who ran an underground fight club. Paula introduced me to him one night—of course without mentioning the fact that they'd been together for two years. He got me into fighting by telling me I could make good money. I thought if I earned enough I could take care of myself and help out at home."

"You picked a heck of a way to do it."

"No kidding. But at seventeen I was six foot four and cocky as hell—the perfect candidate for underground fighting. I did pretty well for myself . . . and for Paula's boyfriend, Angel. I kept it up until I was eighteen and a senior in high school, when my mom had a heart attack and passed away."

Kate's eyes filled with sympathy. "That must have been hard on you and your sister."

The truth was, he still didn't like to think about that time in his life. One of the reasons he'd gotten into fighting was to lighten the load for his mother, but no amount of money could reverse years of stress and overwork on top of high blood pressure. "It was. I was all Tina had after Mom was gone, and I was afraid DSS would come and take her away. But I was making enough money to pay the rent, so I figured if I kept doing what I was doing, we'd manage all right. Until the night Angel told me to throw a fight."

"My God. That really happens?"

"It happened to me. But because I was a teenager full of piss and vinegar, I didn't do it. I won that fight, and ten minutes after it was over Angel and a few of his friends gave me a broken jaw, three broken ribs, and a punctured lung. Paula visited me in the hospital just long enough to spit in my face and tell me how things were with her and Angel."

Kate looked horrified. "Oh, Ian."

He shook his head. "Don't waste any sympathy on me. I was stupid and I got what I deserved. It's just dumb luck I didn't end up in jail, or worse. Dumb luck, and a guidance counselor at school who convinced me not to throw my life away. He made sure I graduated, and then he hooked me up with a city scholarship program so I could go to college." He shrugged. "I majored in business and communications, and the rest, as they say, is history."

There was silence between them for a moment. Then: "What happened to Tina?"

"Tina did well. She went into foster care with a nice couple in Brooklyn, not far from where we'd grown up. She joined the Marines after she graduated from high school and flew helicopters in Iraq. She went to Afghanistan after that, where she met Jacob's father. They got married the next time they were on leave, and when her enlistment was up she got out. She was six months pregnant when Joe was killed in action."

"So Jacob never knew his father."

"No. But he was a good man, a father to be proud of. Jacob will always have that."

There was a crease between Kate's brows. Was she thinking that he hadn't had a father to be proud of—or any father at all?

He hoped not. He didn't want Kate feeling sorry for him, especially since he didn't merit any sympathy. He'd obviously done extremely well for himself, and he'd always viewed pity as a waste of time—whether for himself or for someone else.

"How did Tina die?" she asked softly.

"Drunk driver." He shook his head. "Talk about irony. She made it through two wars without a scratch and ended up getting killed in White Plains by some guy running a red light."

When he realized his hands had clenched into fists, he forced himself to relax. A year had gone by since his sister's death, but the loss still felt like an open wound.

After she'd settled in White Plains, he'd gone over most Sundays to visit. Tina usually made lasagna for dinner—the comfort food of their childhood.

He hadn't eaten lasagna since the night she died.

He didn't want to talk about this anymore. Kate didn't ask anything else, for which he was grateful. After a moment she put her hand on his arm and traced over the tattoos there.

Her touch was soothing and exciting at the same time.

"You could have had these removed," she said after a while, and he was glad she was letting the subject of his sister drop. "Why didn't you?"

"I thought about it, but I didn't want to erase my past. I don't talk about it and I don't display the evidence, but that doesn't mean I'm ashamed of it."

"Ashamed? You should be proud. I can't believe what you accomplished, considering the odds stacked against you."

He shrugged off the compliment and changed the subject. "What about you? Any secrets in your past you'd care to reveal?"

She shook her head. "I'd be embarrassed to tell you about my childhood after hearing about yours. It was so . . . ordinary."

"I don't think any childhood is ordinary. And it's hard to believe yours was, considering you're one of the least ordinary people I've ever met."

In the light of the lamp they'd never bothered to turn off, he could see the blush that came into her cheeks.

"Well, thanks. Maybe *ordinary* isn't the right word, but it was comfortable. Although I was *not* born with a silver spoon in my mouth," she added. "My parents are both teachers, so we were never rich—but we had everything we needed."

"Your grandparents must have been rich, though."

"Eventually. But my grandfather came from a poor family, and my grandmother's family came to this country after World War II with nothing at all."

"Where was your grandmother during the war?"

"In a concentration camp."

He stared at her. "Jesus. Now I really feel like a shit for that silver-spoon comment."

She smiled. "It's okay. She met my grandfather here, and they fell in love and had a wonderful life together. They bought this place with the money my grandfather made as a civil engineer, and my grandmother had a successful career as a photographer."

"What was her name?"

"Rachel Goldman."

His jaw dropped. "Are you kidding? Rachel Goldman was your grandmother?"

She looked pleased. "You've heard of her?"

"Of course I have. I saw her retrospective exhibit at the Museum of Modern Art."

"And here I thought you were a philistine."

"Nice."

She grinned at him. "Anyway, that's my family history in a nutshell."

"Were you raised Jewish?"

"Not really. My father isn't Jewish, and we were pretty non-denominational growing up. We celebrated both Hanukkah and Christmas, which of course my brothers and I thought was great."

"More presents?"

"Exactly."

"Where are your parents now? And your three brothers?"

"My parents still live in Boston, along with one of my brothers. My older brother lives in Michigan, and the youngest is in grad school out in California."

"How come you were the one who ended up with this apartment?"

"I was the only one living in New York, and my grandparents knew I wanted to settle here. So they left the apartment to me, and their money and other assets went to the rest of the family."

She paused and ran the tip of her finger down his nose, and the affectionate intimacy of the gesture made him smile.

"Is there anything else you want to know?" she asked.

"I think that covers your family. But what about you? There must be something embarrassing in your past. Do you have a hidden tattoo anywhere?" He let a wolfish gleam come into his eyes. "Maybe I should look for one."

She shook her head. "No tattoos. When I turned eighteen I thought about getting my grandmother's serial number tattooed on my arm, like hers had been, because I knew some relatives of Holocaust survivors had done that. But she asked me not to. She said that since I was a storyteller, I had other ways to honor the memory of what people had endured in the camps."

He thought about that. "Did you ever write about the Holocaust?"

"I did. The first thing I ever published was a short story set in Auschwitz."

"I didn't know that."

"I haven't written anything like it since. After my grandmother read it, she said it was heartbreaking and true—the highest compliment she could give—but she didn't think I needed to write about the war anymore. She thought my natural inclination was to create more joyful stories."

He remembered *Life with Max*. "I think she was right. You're a natural optimist."

"So was my grandmother, believe it or not. She was an amazing woman."

"I believe it."

Kate yawned suddenly, covering her mouth with her hand. "I think I could fall asleep again."

"You should," he said gently, reaching out to pull her against his chest. Feeling her naked body pressed against his made him feel anything but sleepy, but he managed to tamp down the flash of desire.

A few minutes later, her breathing had turned deep and even. Ian lay watching her in a silence that seemed charmed, almost magical. After a while his eyes closed and he fell asleep with Kate in his arms.

It was the sweetest feeling he'd ever known.

Chapter Nine

But when he woke up, everything was different. Or maybe it would have been more accurate to say that nothing was different.

He felt the same urge to get away he always did the morning after. Even looking at Kate, beautiful as an angel in sleep, didn't make him want to stay.

Her bedroom had felt perfect last night, but now the rose-colored walls and silk curtains seemed suffocatingly feminine.

Everything had become an irritant. His skin was clammy with dried sweat, and his mouth tasted sour. The sun coming through the windows was too bright. The bed was too soft. Kate's comforter was too warm.

And he'd talked too damn much last night.

Remembering their late-night conversation made him feel raw and exposed. What the hell had he been thinking? Why had he told Kate the pathetic story of his misspent youth? If he knew anything about women, the knowledge would make her possessively maternal—as though she could make up for the pain in his past by nurturing him now.

Kate had rolled away during the night and was no longer lying on his arm or against his shoulder. He could easily slip out of bed without waking her.

And then—what? Sneak out of her apartment without a word? Classy.

Not that he hadn't done it before. But that was usually after a one-night stand with a woman he never expected—or wanted—to see again. Kate deserved a hell of a lot more than that.

But he couldn't stay. His urge to be gone was growing stronger by the minute.

Maybe he could leave her a note or send her a text telling her he hadn't wanted to wake her. Then he could mention that since she was picking Jacob up after school on Tuesday, he'd see her that night.

The more he thought about it, the more he liked the idea. He wouldn't be blowing her off, but he wouldn't be sending relationship signals, either.

Although, come to think of it, he had no reason to think Kate would want a relationship with *him*. In fact, it was pretty damn arrogant to assume it. She'd just broken up with her fiancé, after all. Maybe she'd feel the same way he did about last night: it was great rebound sex, but nothing more.

He'd just reached that point in his thoughts when Kate stirred, yawned, and opened her eyes.

"Good morning," she said, smiling at him.

"Good morning."

She rolled onto her back and rubbed her eyes. The movement made the comforter slip down her body, and the sight of her naked breasts and perfect pink nipples caused his body to harden and tighten.

No. No morning sex. That would just muddy the waters.

He sat up and swung his legs over the side of the bed, grabbing his jeans and boxers off the floor. Once he was decent, he turned to face Kate.

She was lying on her side and smiling at him, and she looked so warm and inviting and sexy, he was tempted to pull his clothes right off again.

Instead he leaned over and kissed her on the cheek.

"I had a great time last night," he said, wincing at the inanity of the statement.

"Me, too," Kate said. She sat up and stretched, and he had to look away.

Then she got out of bed, padding over to her closet and grabbing a sky-blue cotton robe.

By the time she turned around, he'd managed to recover from the sight of her perfect ass.

"What would you like for breakfast?" she asked. "It's my favorite meal of the day, so I'm pretty well stocked. I can do an omelet, waffles, bacon, eggs—whatever you want."

It sounded delicious. But staying for breakfast would definitely send the wrong message.

He cleared his throat. "That all sounds great—but I've actually got to go. I'm meeting a friend at the gym for some basketball."

It was sort of the truth. He and Mick usually did play on Sunday mornings, although it wasn't a formal commitment.

He braced himself for Kate's disappointment, but she just nodded. "Sure, no problem. I'll make you breakfast some other time."

A reference to the future. That was bad, but now wasn't the time to deal with it.

"Okay." He hesitated for a moment and then left her room to find his shirt.

It was on the sofa in the living room. Seeing it there made him remember going down on Kate last night, and how incredible it had been to feel her coming apart beneath him.

He forced himself to focus on getting dressed. After he had his shirt and shoes on, Kate came up behind him, wrapping her arms around his waist and kissing the back of his neck.

"Can I make you some coffee before you go?"

"Thanks, but I've got to head out. I'm already running late," he added, in spite of the fact that he had no idea what time it was.

He glanced down at the game on her coffee table.

"You can leave it here if you like," Kate said.

He shook his head and started putting everything back in the box. Leaving something behind would also send the wrong message.

Gallifrey jumped up on the coffee table and looked at him reproachfully.

Of course that was just his imagination. Gallifrey was a cat, and he had no way of knowing that Ian was about to slink out of Kate's apartment with no intention of returning.

Not that he didn't want to see Kate again. He did want to see her again. He wanted her in Jacob's life, and his life, too. As a friend.

He only hoped they could make the transition back to friendship after last night.

Of course, he should have thought of that before he'd slept with her. But his desire for Kate had been stronger than every other instinct. Even now, he couldn't regret giving in to it.

It was the best sex he'd ever had. And unlike Kate, he had a lot to compare it with.

"All right, so . . . I guess I'll see you Tuesday. You're still picking Jacob up after school, right?"

"That's the plan," Kate said, her voice sounding happy and relaxed.

That was both good and bad—good because there wouldn't be an ugly scene right now, bad because an ugly scene might still be looming in their future.

Well, he'd deal with that when—and if—it happened. Maybe once Kate's afterglow faded, she'd realize she'd just been rebounding with him. Maybe she'd be relieved to find out he wasn't expecting to repeat the experience.

She walked him to the door and tilted her head for a goodbye kiss.

He gave her one, planning to keep it short. But the minute their mouths touched he was lost.

She had to have the same morning breath he did, but maybe they cancelled each other out. Because all he could taste was Kate—hot, sweet, irresistible Kate.

He let the game box fall to the floor and put his hands on her hips, driving her back against the door as he kissed her hard and deep. She made a little, sweet sound in her throat, and just like that he was hard for her.

It seemed like a long, dizzying time before he came to his senses. But he did, finally, pulling back and trying to catch his breath.

Kate looked as dazed as he felt. Her face was flushed and her lips were swollen, and he had to tear his eyes from her to pick up the game he'd dropped.

"Well." His voice came out gruff, and he cleared his throat. "Thanks again for . . . everything."

"My pleasure," Kate said with a sudden grin, and his stomach muscles tightened.

"I'll see you on Tuesday."

"See you Tuesday."

Once her door closed behind him, he practically ran for the elevator.

He went from her place straight to his gym, figuring he could use a workout even if Mick wasn't there. Come to think of it, he couldn't remember when his friend was coming back from his honeymoon. Maybe he was still in Hawaii.

But when Ian pushed open the door to the locker room, Mick was there, getting changed.

"Hey, man. How was the honeymoon?"

Mick grinned. "Fantastic. Married life suits me."

"You do look tan—and smug."

"You'd look smug, too, if you were smart enough to marry a woman like Wendy."

It was nice to see his friend so happy. "Maybe I would."

Ian had a permanent locker so he could keep workout gear here. He didn't waste any time getting out of his clothes—they still smelled like Kate, which made him feel tense and aroused at the same time—and into shorts and a tee shirt.

"Are you up for some basketball?" he asked Mick.

"Sounds good."

It was a more-than-usually hard-fought game, and Ian relished the intense focus that sports always brought out in him. It helped to drive out thoughts of Kate, just as the sweat that soaked his tee shirt and stung his eyes helped drown out her scent and the memory of her hands on his skin.

After they called it quits, Ian took a hot shower that banished the last traces of her from his body. He felt almost back to normal as he toweled off and dressed in the spare khakis and polo shirt he kept in his locker.

"You looked good out there," he told Mick as they walked out together.

"Yeah? Well, you looked like you had some kind of demon on your tail. What the hell is up with you?"

Ian stopped walking. "What do you mean? Why do you think something's up?"

Mick stopped walking, too. "Are you kidding? I've known you since we were twelve years old. I know when something's bothering you."

It was true. Mick was his oldest friend. They'd met when they'd joined the Dungeons & Dragons club in junior high, and they'd gone on to play basketball together. They'd stayed friends when he moved to the Bronx and even during his asshole phase, in spite of the fact that he'd burned a lot of bridges during those years. And when they'd ended up at the same college, their friendship had been solidified for good.

"I haven't had coffee yet," he said gruffly. It was an oblique response, but Mick seemed to understand.

"The diner up the street?"

"Yeah."

A few minutes later they were sitting at a Formica table with steaming mugs of coffee in front of them. Mick had ordered breakfast, but Ian didn't feel like eating.

"It's not a big deal," he said as the waitress walked away. "I just slept with a woman last night."

"Not an unusual occurrence for you."

"Yeah, I know."

He hesitated, and after a moment Mick raised an eyebrow. "So what made this different?"

Deciding there was no point in pretending it wasn't, Ian found himself telling Mick about Kate. How he'd worked with her for two years, how he'd cancelled her show, how he'd come to her rescue that night at the club . . . and everything that had happened afterwards.

"Huh," Mick said when he finished. He took a bite of his scrambled eggs and chewed thoughtfully for a minute. "One thing comes to mind," he said after he'd swallowed.

Ian took a gulp of coffee. "Just one?"

"Do you remember back in eighth grade, when we couldn't find a single girl who was interested in playing Dungeons & Dragons? You said if you ever met one, you'd marry her."

He almost spit out his coffee. "For God's sake, Mick. I can't hear something like that on an empty stomach."

"So have a piece of my toast."

Ian sat back and dragged a hand through his hair. "I've got to let her down easy, that's all. I just . . . don't want to lose her friendship. And Jacob likes her so much." He looked at Mick. "I really screwed this up, didn't I?"

His friend shrugged. "Not necessarily. Kate sounds like a reasonable woman. If it really matters to you, you'll find a way to fix things."

He felt a little better. "Maybe you're right." Suddenly hungry, he waved the waitress over.

He ordered pancakes and bacon and grabbed a piece of toast from Mick's plate. "It's good to have you back, man. Do you have pictures from the honeymoon?"

Mick grinned. "Of course. But I'm not going to make you look at them."

"In that case, it's really good to have you back."

∼

He didn't call or text Kate until Tuesday morning, and, to his intense relief, she didn't call or text him, either.

On Tuesday he sent this: *Are you still good to pick up Jacob today?* A few minutes later she replied, *Absolutely! See you tonight.*

Casual and upbeat. So far, so good. Maybe this would be easier than he'd expected.

He felt good all day, and he was still feeling good as he rode the elevator to his apartment after work.

Then he opened his door.

A mouthwatering aroma wafted towards him from the kitchen. Even as his stomach rumbled in anticipation, worry drew his brows together in a frown. A woman cooking in his apartment could mean only one thing.

She was thinking about the future.

Don't jump to conclusions, he told himself as he headed for the kitchen. Maybe she'd just felt like cooking.

Kate stood with her back to him, humming to herself as she stirred something on the stove.

She looked so damn cute in her jeans and a short-sleeved blouse, her feet bare and a kitchen towel tossed over one shoulder. And she really did have the best ass he'd ever seen.

He cleared his throat. "Hey," he said, and Kate turned around.

"Hey!" she said, sounding happy to see him. Then she crossed the space between them, slid an arm around his neck, and gave him a kiss on the lips. "How was work?"

How was work?

It was a girlfriend question. A relationship question.

Not to mention the fact that she'd kissed him hello.

"Fine," he said, avoiding her eyes by walking over to the stove. "What are you making?" he asked, wincing when he heard the words come out of his mouth. That was a relationship question, too.

"Hungarian mushroom soup, chicken casserole, and salad," she said, coming to stand beside him.

She dipped a spoon in the soup, which smelled freaking amazing, and held it out for him to take a sip.

Except that he couldn't.

This whole scene was so domestic, so warm and cozy and casually intimate. His stomach muscles knotted, and a wave of panic rose in his throat.

He backed away from the stove.

Concern filled Kate's blue eyes. "Are you all right?"

He couldn't have The Talk with her right now. Not after she'd cooked this incredible meal and was standing there looking so sweet and beautiful and worried about him.

So he just shook his head. "I feel bad telling you this after you went to so much trouble, but I think I'm coming down with something. It's been coming on all day. My stomach's really off, so I probably shouldn't try to eat anything."

"Of course," she said immediately, and the fact that there wasn't a hint of a pout in her voice or her expression only made him feel worse. "Why don't you go lie down while Jacob and I have dinner? I can make you some tea if you'd like, or—"

He couldn't let her do anything more for him.

"No, that's okay. In fact . . ." He hesitated. "I don't want this to come out the wrong way, but if I know you're here, I won't be able to relax. I'll feel like I should be entertaining you, you know?"

She nodded her comprehension, and her complete lack of injured pique made him feel even lousier. She was so kind and sweet and trusting, and he . . . wasn't.

"I understand. I'll dish up some food for Jacob, put the rest in the fridge, and then head out. Okay?"

He could hardly look at her. "Okay."

She rose up on her toes to give him a kiss on the cheek. "Go lie down," she told him. "Try to get some sleep. I'll be out of here in a few minutes."

"All right. Thanks, Kate."

"Anytime. If I don't see you before then, I'll see you on Friday. If you still want me to pick up Jacob that day?"

He managed a smile. "Sure, that would be great."

"I hope you feel better soon. And if you need anything before Friday, promise you'll give me a call."

"I will."

He went to his room and lay down on his bed. After about ten minutes, he heard the front door open and close, and then he went back out to the kitchen, where Jacob was plowing through the most delicious-looking meal he'd seen in a long time.

"Hey!" his nephew said with his mouth full. "Kate said you weren't feeling good and to let you rest. Are you okay?"

He nodded. "I will be. Are you all set? Do you need anything?"

"I'm great. I told Kate I'd wash the dishes after I eat, so you don't have to worry about it."

Just when he thought he couldn't feel any worse.

"That's nice of you, Jacob. Thanks."

"No problem. Do you want me to bring a tray to your room or anything? This casserole is amazing."

His mouth was watering at the smells that rose from the table, but he shook his head. He couldn't eat the food Kate had cooked after he'd lied to her.

"I'll just make myself a bagel."

"Okay."

As he ate his solitary and unsatisfying meal in his bedroom, Ian acknowledged to himself that he couldn't put off The Talk much longer. Now that he knew it needed to happen, he'd have to make the situation clear to Kate on Friday.

He only hoped he could find a way to do it without hurting her. Or himself.

Chapter Ten

Kate wasn't too surprised that she didn't hear from Ian before Friday, although she was disappointed. But he was sick, after all. And she knew that whatever was happening between them would have to go at Ian's pace.

He was a well-known commitment-phobe—according to the intelligence-gathering operation at the network, anyway—and even if he weren't, he was still a guy. Kate might not be the most man-savvy woman in the world, but she knew enough not to scare Ian off by calling and texting him ten times a day. Not if she wanted a relationship with him.

And she was starting to think she did.

On Saturday night, all she'd thought about was quenching her desire for him. But things between them had been . . .

She didn't have words. And for a writer, that was saying something.

It wasn't just the sex. That had been amazing, but there had been something else between them—something deeper. She hadn't imagined the passion and tenderness and emotion in Ian's eyes, and she knew he'd seen the same thing in hers. Even if he was skittish about relationships, he wouldn't turn his back on that.

But they'd take it slow, for her sake as well as his. It had been only three weeks since Chris had ended their engagement. She wasn't looking to rush things any more than Ian was.

So she didn't worry when she didn't hear from him that week. Besides which, she had other things going on that were just as exciting.

The development executive she'd pitched Jacob's project to had been impressed, and in a follow-up meeting he'd told her that other people at the network were excited as well. They loved the marketing possibilities of a show that had its origins in the imagination of an eleven-year-old boy, and it was starting to look like *Powers* might actually be green-lighted. If so, it would air as an animated series with twelve episodes in the first season and an option for a second season.

When she met Jacob after school on Friday, she could hardly wait to tell him. They went out for ice cream to celebrate, the two of them bubbling over with excitement as if they were both eleven.

"There are still a few hurdles to cross before anything is official, but we might be ready to start negotiating as soon as next week. We can talk to Ian tonight about how he wants to—"

"Do we have to tell him tonight?"

Kate frowned. "Listen, kiddo. If this really happens, we'll be talking money and contracts. You're a minor, and Ian's your legal guardian."

Jacob started playing with his napkin. "I know, but . . . you said it's not official yet."

Kate watched him shred his napkin into several pieces. "Can you tell me why you want to wait? Your uncle loves you—and he's in television. He'll be as excited about this as you are."

Jacob looked up. "No, he won't."

"But—"

"He cancelled your show, didn't he? He told me that's why there won't be new episodes of *Life with Max*."

Was he mad at his uncle on her behalf? She hoped that wasn't the case. Of course, she'd been mad at Ian herself when it had first happened. Furious, even. She always wanted quality and creativity to trump every other factor. But then, it was her job to be creative . . . and it was Ian's job to consider all those other factors.

As much as she hadn't wanted to admit it, a part of her had always understood Ian's decision even as she'd disagreed with it. And she realized now that she'd long since forgiven him for the choices he had to make as an executive—especially since she'd gotten to know the man behind the suit.

"Yes, he cancelled *Life with Max*. But that was a business decision—and probably a good one. The show was popular with its core fans, and I was proud of the work my team did on it, but it wasn't ever going to connect with a wide audience. There are places for niche shows like that, but not on a major network. Your uncle was just doing his job."

Jacob didn't look convinced. "It's not only that. He doesn't like any of the things I like. He doesn't care about what I'm interested in."

"He cares about *you*. And if you give him a chance, you might find out you have more in common than you think."

When she saw him that night, she'd suggest to Ian that he tell his nephew about his Dungeons & Dragons phase. He could even teach him how to play.

Jacob shrugged. "I doubt it."

"But—"

"It doesn't matter. But about the show—you said there are still hurdles to cross, right? I don't want to tell him and sound all excited and then have everything fall through. Can't we wait until it really is official? Please?"

She wished Jacob trusted his uncle more, but that would only come with time. And it was true that the project could still fall through. She'd been in television long enough to know how real that possibility was. Could it hurt to wait until there was an actual offer on the table? That was the point at which Ian had to be involved.

She sighed. "All right. But the minute they start talking turkey, we're telling your uncle. And I promise he'll be as proud and thrilled as you are."

Jacob looked relieved. "Thanks, Kate. So what should we do now?"

"Do you want to go to a comic-book store?"

"Yes!"

∼

They had a wonderful afternoon, made even more wonderful for Kate by the knowledge that she'd be seeing Ian soon.

Every time she thought about him walking through the door, her heart beat faster.

Jacob had said his uncle was over his illness. If Ian really was recovered, and if she was still here after Jacob went to bed, wasn't there a chance the two of them could do some old-fashioned fooling around?

Of course she wouldn't stay the night, not with Jacob in the apartment. But she'd settle for a few long kisses. In fact, as she remembered the effect Ian's kisses had on her, the thought of spending an hour on his terrace in a lip-lock made her knees weak.

She wouldn't count on that, though. Even though Ian was well enough to go to work, he might still be feeling under the weather—and she'd already decided to let him set the pace as far as their relationship went.

But she couldn't stop her excitement from building as afternoon turned to evening. Jacob had disappeared into his room, and she was curled up on the living room couch, trying to read a magazine without much success. Her thoughts kept drifting to Ian, and she found herself smiling into space as she relived their night together.

When her phone rang and she saw his name on the screen, her smile turned into a grin.

"Hey there," she said.

"Hey." There was a short pause, and then, "I've got a huge favor to ask you. If the answer's no, that's completely all right."

Something about dinner, probably. "What's the favor?"

"Is there any way you could stay a little later tonight?"

Pleasure spread through her like warm honey. "I think I could manage that."

"That's great. Is midnight too late? If it is, I can be home sooner."

She blinked and readjusted her ideas. He was asking her to stay *for* him, not *with* him.

Well, why not? They could fool around when he got back, couldn't they?

"Midnight would be fine. Is it a work thing or a friend thing?"

Another pause. "Actually, it's a date thing."

For a moment it just didn't register. Date thing? What did he mean? Not that he was going on a date with another woman. That couldn't be.

"Do you mean . . . what do you mean?"

Maybe it was an obligation kind of date. Like he'd promised to escort a female friend somewhere, or bring a date to a network event, or something. And of course if it was a network event, he wouldn't invite her. That would be awkward.

"A woman I met at the gym asked if I wanted to go for a drink."

A woman he'd met at the gym. Asked him out for a drink.

And he'd said yes.

Slowly, very slowly, the reality of the situation sank in.

Ian was going on a date with another woman. And he was asking *her* to babysit. While he bought this woman drinks, and flirted with her, and kissed her good night.

Or more. If he took her back to her place by nine or ten o'clock, that would leave plenty of time for more.

And she knew firsthand how good Ian Hart was at talking a woman into bed.

Her silence had lasted way too long. She had to say something.

Her mouth opened, but nothing came out.

He had to know this floored her. He had to have known she would—

And then, suddenly, she understood.

Ian wasn't stupid. He hadn't agreed to go on a date without knowing she would be upset. Ian was a strategic thinker—she knew that from working with him.

Which meant he'd done this deliberately.

This was his way of breaking things off with her. His way of letting her know that what they'd had wouldn't be repeated. While she'd been imagining their next night together, Ian had been thinking about his next one-night stand.

But she couldn't let him know how hurt she was. Her pride demanded that she at least give the pretense of not giving a damn, even if he knew perfectly well that she did.

She took a deep breath. "So, midnight. Midnight will be fine. I'll see you then."

That was all she could manage. Without waiting for Ian to respond, she ended the call.

Tears stung behind her eyelids, but she couldn't cry in the living room. What if Jacob came out of his room and saw her?

She went into the bathroom and locked the door. Then she sank down on the toilet seat and let the tears fall.

Stupid, stupid, stupid.

How could she have been such an idiot? Not to mention such a *girl*. She was like a cautionary tale out of a *Cosmo* article. She'd ignored all the signs that told her Ian was not relationship material, and she'd been willfully blind to every signal he'd sent. She'd built up hope and expectations with absolutely no justification.

But she couldn't blame Ian. What was it he'd said that night? *If you let me be your rebound, I swear you won't regret it.*

He hadn't led her on. He hadn't promised anything beyond that one night. He'd even called himself her rebound.

If she'd gotten hurt, it was her own damn fault. That was the fair way to look at the situation.

But she didn't feel like being fair.

She remembered a fender bender from a few years ago. She hadn't been injured, but she'd woken up the next morning bruised and aching all over.

She felt like that now. Like she'd been beaten up. And, fair or not, she wanted to take it out on Ian. She wanted to hurt him like he'd hurt her.

But a man with Ian's attitude about relationships wasn't susceptible to hurt. There wasn't anything she could do to him that would make him feel like this.

Because he didn't have a heart.

She got up, turned on the faucet, and splashed her face with cold water. Then she toweled herself dry and went back out to the living room.

She'd come full circle as far as Ian went. She'd always thought he didn't have a heart, and now she had proof.

But then her glance fell on the bookcase. When she looked at the bottom shelf, she saw the Dungeons & Dragons set.

She sat down on the couch and closed her eyes.

As much as she wanted to wipe out the last few weeks and go back to her old, two-dimensional image of Ian, she knew she couldn't.

Ian hadn't been pretending with her. The man she'd seen Saturday night was the real thing. Complicated and a little damaged, sure . . . but also passionate and tender and caring.

What she was seeing now was the armor he put on to protect himself from all that.

Kate took a deep breath, opened her eyes, and went into the kitchen to make dinner for herself and Jacob.

She had no reason to feel like an idiot. Ian was the idiot. And in the long run, he'd hurt himself a hell of a lot worse than the women he slept with. They'd get over the momentary pain of being dumped, but Ian was stuck with himself forever.

And it wasn't like she'd gotten nothing from the experience. She'd had the best sex of her life, and a taste of the kind of passion and intimacy she was looking for in the bedroom. Ian wasn't capable of giving that to a woman on a long-term basis, but that didn't mean no man was. She just had to find someone who could make her feel the way Ian did but who was actually capable of commitment.

As impossible as it had seemed just half an hour ago, Kate was starting to think she and Ian could go back to being friends. God knew he needed one, and so did his nephew.

Although she would draw the line at babysitting during dates. She might be exhibiting some impressive emotional maturity here, but she wasn't a martyr. Ian could find someone else to stay with his nephew while he slept his way around Manhattan.

Jacob went to bed at nine thirty, and Kate turned on the TV.

She actually got caught up in a new sci-fi show she hadn't had a chance to watch yet—so much so that when Ian got home, she looked up in surprise.

"Is it midnight already?" she asked, glancing at the clock on the TV. It was only eleven.

She looked back at Ian. "How was your date?"

He stood across the living room from her, looking tense and unhappy.

It was good to know he felt a little guilty. Seeing him so uncomfortable actually made her feel more at ease.

"It couldn't have been *too* good," she went on. "You're home early, after all."

He took a few steps towards her, his expression uncertain. "It was okay," he said after a moment. "How was your night?"

She shrugged. "All right, I guess. Jacob and I had spaghetti for dinner."

"Spaghetti, huh? That sounds good."

He looked like he was waiting for her to strike him dead. She almost felt sorry for him. Had he spent the evening wondering what she was going to do to him when he got back?

The thought made her smile. Emotional maturity, it seemed, was its own reward.

She rose to her feet.

"I guess I'll head home now. I'll see you Tuesday—if you still need me to pick up Jacob after school that day."

His eyes searched hers. "That would be great," he said after a moment. "If you—if you're sure you don't mind."

"Not at all. I'm happy to help you out with your nephew. Although"—*might as well get this out there*—"I'd rather not be your go-to babysitter for date nights. Find someone else for that."

He cleared his throat and looked away. "Yeah, of course. I really appreciate your help tonight, but—yeah. I'll find someone else for . . . if I . . ." His voice trailed off.

"Good," she said briskly, slipping on her shoes and grabbing her purse.

She headed for the door, and he followed her. She turned the knob, then looked back over her shoulder.

"Good night, Ian."

"Good night," he echoed, and then she was out the door.

∼

Ian was in hell.

It had been one of the worst weekends of his life. He would have felt better if Kate had punched him in the face, which he probably deserved.

He'd lied about having a date. He'd spent the evening at the gym, working out like a goddamn lunatic.

He hadn't been able to wait until midnight to go home. Whatever Kate had to say to him, he wanted to get it over with.

And then she'd been . . . great.

A little pissed, obviously. That had been clear when she'd told him that she wouldn't watch Jacob on date nights. Which, of course, was perfectly reasonable.

Her whole attitude had been reasonable. She didn't pretend she was happy about his dating other women, but she didn't punish him for it, either.

He should have been relieved. Kate had let him off the hook, and a hell of a lot sooner than he'd expected or deserved.

Instead, he was miserable.

Was it possible that that was what she'd intended? Was this some kind of Machiavellian plot to make him want her back?

If so, it was working.

But he couldn't believe that Kate was trying to manipulate him. She was too straightforward, too transparently honest.

On Sunday afternoon he took Jacob to the new Spider-Man movie, but he couldn't concentrate on what was happening on the screen. His thoughts kept returning to Kate.

What was she doing now? Had she called Simone to tell her what a prick he was and to make plans to go clubbing?

The thought that she might have hooked up the night before made him want to punch someone—like the guy who'd been lucky enough to go home with her.

He closed his eyes.

Had some man been with Kate last night? Had some man run his hands over that incredible body and seen her heart in those blue eyes?

He scrubbed his face with his hands. What Kate had done or hadn't done with another guy was none of his business. *She* was none of his business.

He'd made sure of that himself.

~

It was a three-day weekend. On Tuesday morning he was back at his desk, but he had a hard time focusing. He was so distracted, he considered cancelling a lunch appointment with a producer who was thinking of leaving a rival network. But he'd never yet let a woman affect his work, and he wouldn't start now.

The lunch confirmed his feelings about the producer, Walter Carey—that he was an untrustworthy weasel who would turn on a new company as easily as he was turning on his current one.

He seemed to think their meeting was going great, though. And he obviously thought he'd be putting the cherry on the sundae by imparting a piece of confidential information.

"You could use a man like me on your side, considering the way your former writers are stabbing you in the back. Of course, I'm sure they feel justified if their shows are cancelled, but it doesn't make it any easier to swallow, right?"

He asked the question with a smirk on his face, obviously expecting Ian's curiosity to be aroused.

Oh, well, what the hell. They'd finished eating, but he still had to wait for the check; they needed some way to pass the time.

"Who's stabbing us in the back?" he asked.

Walter's eyes gleamed.

"This is strictly confidential, obviously. The boys upstairs are pretty excited, but nothing's final yet."

"Yeah?" Ian asked, surreptitiously glancing at his watch. Where the hell was their waiter with the check?

Walter leaned forward across the table. "Kate Meredith pitched a project to us. It's a surefire winner. And get this—apparently she got the idea for it from your nephew."

Ian just stared at him.

He knew his shock was showing on his face, because Walter looked pleased.

"Sure, you guys cancelled her show—but that happens all the time. It takes a stone-cold bitch to get her revenge by pitching an idea she got from your nephew to a rival network."

Oh, God.

It was a hell of a lot worse than this jackass suspected. He hadn't heard a word about this from Jacob, which meant that he didn't know about it, either. So Kate wasn't just pitching an idea she'd gotten from him to Walter's network. She was pitching an idea she'd *stolen* from him.

Jacob wrote stories and drew comics—Ian knew that. Jacob must have showed them to Kate. Had it been then that she'd thought of this way to get her revenge, or had her planning started even further back?

Maybe when he'd asked her to watch Jacob, it had occurred to her that his nephew might be a vulnerable spot. A way to get back at him for cancelling her show.

Or maybe it wasn't about that. Maybe her plan was more recent, and she was getting back at him for breaking her heart—not that she had a heart to break.

"When . . ." He had to clear his throat. "When did Kate come to you with this pitch?"

Walter shrugged. "I'm not sure. I heard about it for the first time yesterday."

Yesterday. It all fit in.

But whether she'd done this to get back at him for cancelling her show or to punish him for Friday night didn't matter. What did matter was the fact that Kate Meredith was manipulative, vindictive, and a first-class liar.

But to involve an eleven-year-old boy in her plot? That took a rare breed of nastiness.

He felt sick.

Boy, he sure could pick them. He'd fallen hook, line, and sinker for Paula, and she'd never given a damn about him. And years later—long after he should have known better—there'd been that actress who'd declared her undying love . . . all the while hoping he'd get her a part on one of his shows.

How could he have been so stupid? He might have great instincts when it came to business, but when it came to women he didn't have a goddamn clue.

He'd better stick to one-night stands.

Unable to look at Walter's self-satisfied face any longer, he shoved his chair back and got to his feet. "I'm going to find our waiter and pay the bill. It's on me, of course. We'll be in touch."

Walter looked a little startled, but he nodded and held out his hand. "I look forward to hearing from you."

Ten minutes later, Ian was striding away from the restaurant with his cell phone in his hand, trying to reach Mick.

"Hello?"

"Thank God. I need a favor. A big one."

"Of course," his friend said immediately. "Whatever you need."

"Can you pick Jacob up from school today? If you can't, I—"

"No, I can do that. The best thing about being a web designer is setting my own hours."

"Thanks, Mick. I owe you."

"Do you want to tell me what's going on?"

He hesitated. "Not really. Not right now. Maybe tonight when I pick up Jacob."

"Okay. I'll see you when I see you."

That was like Mick—helping him out with no questions asked. Thank God there were people like him in the world to make up for the people like Kate.

He checked his watch: one thirty. If he went to her apartment now, he might catch her before she left to pick up Jacob. If not, he'd go to the school and wait for her there.

One way or another, he was going to tell her exactly what he thought of her before the day was over. And then, God willing, he'd never see Kate Meredith again.

Chapter Eleven

Kate was getting ready to go pick up Jacob when her intercom buzzed.

"Yes?"

"Mr. Hart is here. Shall I send him up?"

"Yes, of course."

Why was Ian here? And without calling first? Was something wrong with Jacob?

As soon as she heard the elevator stop at her floor, she pulled the door open.

"What's going on? Is Jacob all right?"

"He's fine—no thanks to you."

She stared at him. He was in a business suit, so he'd come straight from work. His eyes were narrow and his jaw was tight.

"What are you talking about? What on earth is wrong with you?"

He took a step closer to her and then stopped, stuffing his hands in his pockets as though stifling an urge to wring her neck.

"How could you do that to Jacob?"

She was completely bewildered. "Do what to Jacob?"

"Pitch an idea to a network that you stole from him."

Her head jerked back as though he'd slapped her. He'd found out about *Powers*, obviously—and this was the conclusion he'd drawn.

"You think I stole an idea from your nephew? You think I could do that?"

"I didn't until today. You really did a job on me, Kate. I was starting to think you were different." He shook his head. "I was wrong."

"Ian, listen to me. I did pitch an idea to another network, but—"

"Spare me," he said, his voice cold. "I don't want to hear it. I just came up here to tell you to stay away from Jacob—and from me."

He meant it. He wasn't going to give her a chance to explain—and he obviously hadn't bothered to get the true story from Jacob before he'd come over here.

A hot wave of anger burned away her confusion and hurt.

"That's what you came up here for?"

"Yeah."

"Well, then, I guess that's it. Have a nice life."

He stared at her. "Is that all you have to say for yourself?"

She laughed shortly. "I thought you didn't want to hear anything from me. But if I'm allowed to speak, then yes, I do have something to say."

She took a step towards him. "You're a smart man, Hart. You have good instincts—sometimes. You should use those instincts to compare the person you know I am with what you just accused me of. Then ask yourself if it makes any damn sense."

She took a breath. "I know you've been betrayed before. Paula used you and almost got you killed, and I'm sure you've had other shitty experiences with women. I get that, and I feel sorry for you."

He flinched.

"But nothing anyone ever did to you gives you the right to hurt someone else. You think you're the only person in the world who's been let down or betrayed? My grandmother was a Holocaust survivor, for God's sake. There's not a person on the planet who would have blamed her if she'd turned her back on the human race. But she didn't. She made a life for herself and her family. She used to say that you can look forward with love or backward with hate, and people have to make that choice for themselves. But holding on to bitterness is like drinking poison and waiting for someone else to die, and she by God wasn't going to waste her time like that."

He started to speak, but she held up a hand. "I only have one more thing to say. When you talk to Jacob about this, you're going to find out that you were wrong. That you behaved like an ass and lashed out at me for no reason. You're going to feel really bad about it, and you'll probably want to apologize. So let me save you the trouble in advance." She lifted her chin. "*I don't want to hear it.* I don't give a damn about your apology. I don't want to see you or hear from you ever again. I'd still like to spend time with Jacob, but if that's going to happen, it'll be up to you to manage it without us having contact. Goodbye, Hart."

She turned on her heel and went back into her apartment, slamming the door behind her. Then she went into her bathroom, turned the water on full force, stripped off her clothes, and stepped into the shower.

She was so mad she could spit, so it was a good thing she was standing over a drain.

∼

A little while later she was dressed again and pacing back and forth across her living room. The shower hadn't calmed her down, and neither had stalking around her apartment like a caged tiger.

She texted Simone.

I need you. Code red. Where are you?

Her answer came in less than a minute.

Watching rehearsal. I'm sitting in the back of the house.

Half an hour later, her taxi pulled up in front of the theater. She could hear the rehearsal in progress from the lobby, so she went through the door as quietly as possible.

Simone was sitting in the back row watching the actors onstage. As soon as she saw Kate, she slipped out of her seat and came to meet her.

"Is this a bad time?" Kate whispered.

Simone shook her head. "No, it's fine. I've got an hour or so before they'll need me. Do you want to grab a coffee?"

Kate nodded. She was just about to open the door, when a strong baritone voice called out from the middle of the house, stopping the action. She paused, watching as a tall male figure strode down the aisle and went up on the stage, talking to the actors.

It was Zach Hammond. Kate stared at the impossibly handsome man for a long moment, and then turned to Simone.

"He's like a Greek god or something."

Simone ran both hands through her short hair. There must have been some product in it, because when she was done it stood on end.

She looked like she'd been electrocuted. "I know. Let's get out of here."

Clearly Simone was dealing with some issues of her own, but Kate decided hers had priority. She started talking in the lobby and she didn't stop until they'd gotten their drinks at Starbucks and sat down at an outside table.

When she was done, Simone nodded slowly. "Okay. Here are my thoughts." She paused. "First, what a dick."

Kate felt a fresh wave of anger. "I know."

"Second, why the hell didn't you tell me you guys slept together last week?"

Kate blinked. Then, to buy time, she took a sip of her latte. It was too hot, and she burned her tongue.

"I'm not sure," she said after a moment. "I mean . . . there's no particular reason."

"You can do better than that."

"Oh, all right." She sighed. "I guess I was afraid you'd think . . ." Her voice trailed off.

Simone frowned. "You couldn't have thought I'd judge you. You know my track record with guys."

Kate shook her head. "I didn't think that. I knew if I told you I'd had rebound sex with Ian, you'd be all for it. The problem was, it was more than that to me. I couldn't separate the sex from the feelings I had when we were having sex." She paused. "That's kind of a confusing sentence, but you know what I mean. And that was the part I was afraid to tell you. I'd just broken up with Chris, and Ian obviously isn't relationship material. I thought you'd say—"

"That you should stop being a hopeless romantic and just be happy you finally had great sex?"

She slumped down in her chair. "Yes."

"It's not too late to do that, you know. I mean, yes, Ian has proved himself to be a total asshole, but you can still be happy you had great sex. You're no worse off than if you'd never seen him again after that night."

"It's not that simple. There's Jacob, for one thing."

"That's a little tricky, sure. But that part's not up to you. Ian's his guardian; if he wants Jacob to spend time with you, he'll have to make that happen within the boundaries you set."

"I suppose you're right."

Simone looked at her shrewdly. "But that's not all you're thinking about, is it?"

Kate covered her face with her hands. "I can't look at you."

"Are you kidding? Kate, this is me. You held my hair back while I puked in the parking lot sophomore year. We've seen each other at our best and our worst. You can tell me anything."

Kate looked up. "I think . . . I still . . . have feelings for him." She went on quickly. "Of course, I won't act on them. I have too much self-respect to do that to myself. It's just . . ."

"You can't change the way you feel."

She nodded.

The two of them sat in silence for a moment, drinking their coffee and watching the people walking past. That was one of the great things about living in New York: there was so much life happening around you at any given moment that it was easy to distract yourself from your own pathetic existence.

After a while Kate sighed. "Do you remember what I said that night at the club?"

"You said a lot of things. Which one, exactly?"

"I said I was sick of being the well-meaning idiot everyone feels sorry for. I said I was sick of thinking about everyone but myself."

"And?"

"And here I am again. I guess character really is destiny."

Simone folded her arms. "Okay, let's get one thing straight. It's not a character flaw to be a decent, loving, forgiving person. It's only a flaw if you let people walk all over you, and you haven't done that. In fact, it sounds to me like you scorched Ian Hart pretty damn thoroughly."

Kate thought about it. "I guess I did."

"Hell, yes, you did. So don't beat yourself up for your feelings. We can't control the way we feel; we can only control the way we act. And you've done that."

"Maybe you're right."

"I'm always right."

Kate grinned suddenly. "Yeah? That reminds me—speaking of feelings we can't control, how is it working with Zach Hammond?"

She'd never seen her friend blush like that before.

"Wow. You've got it bad, huh?"

"I don't want to talk about it," Simone muttered.

"I'm telling you, that man could be a movie star."

"Very funny."

"But of course, if he doesn't do it for you, he doesn't. Not everyone reacts to—"

"Will you please shut up?"

Kate shook her head but let the subject drop. Simone wouldn't be able to keep a lid on her feelings for long. Eventually there'd be a late-night phone call and Kate would hear everything. They'd taken turns supporting each other for ten years now, and she hoped they'd keep doing it for the next fifty.

That was the nice thing about best friends: unlike men, you could always count on them.

As though her last thought had been a cue, her phone rang. When she saw Chris's name, she sighed.

"This'll just take a sec," she told Simone, before getting up and walking a few paces away.

"Hi, Chris. What's up?"

"Hi, Kate." A short pause. "I just . . . I need to apologize. For Anastasia, for that day at your apartment . . . for everything."

"It's okay." And as she said it, she realized it was true. She didn't want Chris back in her life, but she forgave him.

The split between them had been for the best. They'd been together because it was easy, not because it was right. They both deserved better than that.

"Thanks. I was hoping maybe we could have a drink or something. Not because I want to get back together," he added quickly. "The truth is, I think I should spend some time alone. But I'd like a chance to say goodbye to you. Goodbye and thank you."

They'd been together for eight months. Getting closure would be good for both of them.

"Sure. We can do that. Why don't you come by my place tomorrow night? We can have a drink at the bar on the corner."

"That sounds great. Seven o'clock?"

"I'll see you then."

As she sat back down at the table, she reflected on the turn her life had taken. It had been less than a month since Chris had slept with another woman and broken their engagement, and she'd come to terms with her feelings and moved on.

Now she just had to come to terms with her feelings for Ian . . . and move on.

∼

It was raining cats and dogs and Ian didn't have an umbrella, but he didn't care. He had to apologize to Kate, and if that meant waiting in the rain until he grew gills, then that was what he'd do.

He'd been in the doorway of the building across the street for the last twenty minutes. She hadn't answered any of his calls—no surprise there—and when he went to her apartment, Andreas told him that she'd gone out about an hour before.

So he'd wait for her to come back. No matter how long it took.

She'd been right about everything.

As soon as he'd gotten home the day before, he'd talked to Jacob, and his nephew had told him the whole story.

"Kate wanted to tell you right away, but I wouldn't let her. I know you think comics and superheroes are stupid. I wanted to wait until everything was settled before I told you. That way you wouldn't be able to laugh at me or tell me to go play football or something."

Jacob's expression had been angry and miserable. It was obvious that Kate had been right the night of Mick's wedding, when she'd accused him of trying to turn Jacob into someone he wasn't.

He couldn't even think about trying to fix things with Kate until he'd fixed things with Jacob.

"Would you let me read your story? I'd really like to."

At first Jacob said no, but when Ian asked again, his nephew agreed, albeit grudgingly. Jacob brought the book out into the living room, handed it to him without a word, and then went back to his room and shut the door.

Ian was blown away.

He'd had no idea his nephew was capable of something like this. The story was rough, of course, but it was exciting and original and compelling. He wasn't surprised that Kate had recognized that fact immediately.

He didn't try to push too hard with Jacob that night. He knocked on his door, handed the book back, and told him it was fantastic.

"Whatever. Did you apologize to Kate?"

"I will tomorrow. I promise."

Now, standing across the street from her apartment in the dubious shelter of an archway, he wondered if she'd ever talk to him again.

She'd been pretty clear on that point yesterday. But Kate had a generous heart, and he was counting on that heart to give him a second chance.

Not that he deserved one.

There was a café next door to Kate's building. Did his guilt demand that he go without coffee?

He decided that coffee could be allowed during his vigil. He'd get it to go and keep an eye out to make sure he didn't miss Kate.

He turned up the collar of his overcoat—not that it did much to shield him from the driving rain—and went to the crosswalk.

He froze.

The blare of a car horn brought him back to his senses, and he made it back to the sidewalk without getting run over.

Kate was in the bar on the corner. She was sitting at a table by the window . . . with Chris.

In one split second he went from a sane, reasonable, penitent human being to some kind of caveman fueled by a wave of jealousy so powerful it made him shake.

Slowly, painfully, he forced himself to calm down.

What the hell was she doing with that jerk?

Awareness of the irony wasn't far behind. Chris might be a jerk, but Ian was worse.

Rebound sex was supposed to help you move on after a breakup. But what if he'd been such an asshole that he'd driven Kate back into her ex-fiancé's arms?

For the first time that night, he was grateful for the rain. It was cold and bleak and mirrored his mood.

It was what he deserved.

He wanted to go into that bar and break Chris's jaw. But in a contest to pick the biggest jerk in Kate's life, it would be a toss-up between the two of them. Chris had just as much reason to break his jaw.

So he went back to his doorway. He couldn't see them anymore, but he had a clear view of the bar's front door. He'd know when they came out.

And if they went back to her place together.

He didn't have long to wait. Ten minutes later, they came through the door, saw the rain, and retreated under the shelter of the bar's awning. They stood talking together for several minutes.

Ian shoved his hands into his pockets so he wouldn't try to tear chunks of stone out of the wall behind him.

It was obviously a friendly conversation; Kate's body language was comfortable and relaxed. After a little while Chris said something that made her laugh, and then they hugged.

Ian tensed. Was that a goodbye-and-good-luck hug, or a first-step-on-the-road-to-reconciliation hug?

He felt a surge of relief when they separated, Chris hailing a cab and Kate hurrying down the sidewalk with her shoulders hunched against the rain. Even if they were thinking about getting back together, at least they weren't together yet.

Suddenly he realized what he'd just tacitly admitted to himself.

He hadn't come here just to apologize. He'd come to ask Kate to be with him.

As in date. As in exclusively. As in the thing he never did.

Of course, she'd be crazy to agree. Any friend who had her best interests at heart would tell her so. But that wouldn't stop him from trying.

He waited until Andreas let her in, and then he crossed the street.

"Good timing, sir. Ms. Meredith just got back."

"Thanks," he said, making sure that Kate had gone up in the elevator before he entered the lobby.

A few minutes later he was standing outside her apartment, his heart going a million miles an hour. He was also dripping on the hallway floor, but he didn't give a damn about that. All he could think about was the woman on the other side of this door.

He took a deep breath and knocked.

When the door opened, Kate was there with a smile, toweling off her hair. When she saw who it was, the smile faded. "I thought you were Chris," she said, her eyes turning cold and distant.

Maybe when Chris had hailed a cab, it had been to go home and pick up his pajamas and toothbrush.

The thought made his stomach clench. "Are you expecting him? Is he . . . staying here tonight?"

She stared at him. "Are you kidding? Do you honestly think that's any of your business? Go away, Hart."

She started to close the door, but he stepped across the threshold before she could.

Her eyes narrowed. "In two seconds I'm going to scream bloody murder and call the cops."

"It's about Jacob," he said, knowing that was the only thing in the world he could say right now that she might listen to.

She sighed. "All right, fine. You have one minute."

It was a start. "Jacob asked me to tell you that he wants to go ahead with *Powers* if you're still interested."

"You can tell Jacob I'll send him an email tomorrow to touch base." She paused. "I take it you're okay with this now?"

"Yeah."

Her lip curled. "Then you and Jacob must have talked."

"Yeah."

"I'm glad for his sake. But if you have anything else to say, I don't need to hear it."

He reached for her hand before he could stop himself. "Please, Kate."

She jerked her hand away. "I told you yesterday I'm not interested in your apology."

"I'll get on my knees if I have to."

"Oh, really?" Her expression was skeptical. "I think it'll be a cold day in hell before I see Ian Hart—"

He didn't even hesitate. He dropped to his knees and reached for her hand again.

"Kate, I'm so sorry. I jumped to conclusions, and I was wrong. There's no excuse for my behavior, and I won't try to give you one. I'll just say that if you give me another chance to be in your life, I won't screw it up."

Her eyes widened. For a moment after he finished speaking, she just stared at him. Then she shook her head sharply, pulled her hand from his grasp, and backed up a few steps.

"No. No way. I'm not letting you in again."

He rose to his feet. "Kate—"

She ran both hands through her damp hair. The action made him aware for the first time of what she was wearing—a short-sleeved blouse and a knee-length skirt that the rain had plastered to her body. When she raised her arms, her breasts strained against the material.

A flash of lust lanced through him.

He shook his head to clear it and tried again. "Kate—"

"Save it, Hart. It wasn't enough that you seduced me and then rejected me—which I dealt with like a damn saint. But then you had to push me even further away. You needed to invent a whole betrayal scenario to do it, but that didn't stop you."

Her lips trembled for a moment before she went on. "The sad thing is, I actually blamed myself for that first situation. I thought I'd made the same mistake women have been making for centuries: reading more into sex than was ever there. I thought I'd been blind and stupid."

"Kate—"

"But *you* were the blind one. *You* were the stupid one. Because there was more between us than we expected, not less. And you ran away from that like the gutless coward you are."

There was a long beat of silence. When Kate spoke again, her voice was quieter.

"Look, Hart—I'm sorry Paula hurt you so badly. But you don't have to expect every woman you meet to be like her. You could expect them to be like your mother and Tina."

He laughed shortly. "Yeah? They left me, too."

As soon as the words were out of his mouth, he regretted them. He didn't blame his mother and Tina for dying. What the hell kind of thing was that to say? Was that really lurking in his subconscious somewhere?

He rubbed a hand over his face. What was it about Kate that made him reveal himself like this? Now she'd think he was even more screwed up than she already did.

"They didn't leave you on purpose," Kate said gently. "They died."

"Yeah, I know. Forget I said that, okay? I don't know where that came from."

"You miss them."

He dropped his hand to his side. "Goddamn it, Kate, stop looking at me like that."

Her eyes were as gentle as her voice. "Like what?"

"Like you feel sorry for me."

She tilted her head to the side, and a lock of hair fell across her cheek. "I do feel sorry for you. That's not the worst thing in the world."

"It is to me. Damn it, you're doing it again."

She threw up her hands. "How do you want me to look at you?"

Her words hung in the air for a moment. Then he closed the distance between them and pushed her back against the wall.

He leaned in close and felt her shiver. "I want you to look at me like you did Saturday night. Like you did the day Chris was here and I held you just like this." His jaw tensed. "I saw you with him at that bar, and it made me crazy. I couldn't handle it, thinking you'd gone back to that asshole—"

"Chris isn't an asshole," Kate said. Her voice was trembling. "He has a lot of good qualities."

"Oh yeah? Name one."

"He's . . . he's . . . gentle."

His grip on her shoulders tightened. "I'm not gentle."

She closed her eyes. "No."

"Is that a problem for you?"

He watched the heat creep into her face. "No."

"I didn't think so," he whispered. Her eyes fluttered open and she stared at him, her breath quick and shallow.

He moved his hands to her hips. "I've wanted to take you against a wall since that night at the club." He smoothed his palms down her thighs. "The day Chris was here, I was a breath away from doing it." He found the hem of her skirt, and his hands slid underneath and up her bare legs.

She drew in a sharp breath. "Ian . . . stop. You have to stop."

He did, but he didn't pull back.

"Are you saying you don't want me?"

Kate turned her head away. "After everything that's happened between us, I should hate you."

"That isn't what I asked."

She met his eyes again, and there was turmoil in her expression. But behind her anger and confusion and uncertainty, he saw an unmistakable spark of desire.

He began to stroke her bare thighs again, letting his hands rove higher until he found the edge of her panties.

He traced that edge softly, slowly, his fingertips grazing over the sensitive crease where her leg met her hip.

"Ian..."

There was a pleading note in her voice. He wasn't sure if she was begging him to stop or to keep going, but he was going to assume the latter.

He covered her mound with his palm.

She gasped and clutched at his shoulders. He massaged her through her panties, and the little sounds she made had him hungry for more.

He slipped a finger underneath the soft lace, and she was so hot and wet and ready for him, he almost howled like a wolf.

"Kate—"

She squirmed against him, and he slicked a finger back and forth over her clitoris.

"Ian!"

Her face was flushed, her eyes bright.

"What do you want, Kate?"

"I want... I want—"

"Tell me, sweetheart."

"I want you inside me. Now."

He was already hard, but that turned him into an iron rod.

"You're sure?" he said thickly.

"Yes. Yes..."

Christ, he hoped there was a condom in his wallet.

He kept one hand on Kate's glorious heat as he pulled out his wallet with the other. Yes, thank God—a single foil packet.

He held it in his teeth as he dropped the wallet to the floor. Only then did he pull away from Kate, but just so he could shrug out of his overcoat, undo his pants, and push them down far enough to free his erection.

"Panties," he growled as he tore open the condom and rolled it over his shaft.

As orders went, it was a little vague, but Kate had no trouble interpreting it. She wriggled them off and kicked them away, and then he hooked his hand under her right thigh to hoist her leg over his hip.

She was ready for him—and God knew he was ready for her. But as he gazed down into her flushed, sweet, beautiful face, he hesitated.

He wanted her physically more than he'd ever wanted a woman. But with Kate, it wouldn't be just physical. He showed himself to her in ways he didn't expect. And when she revealed herself to him, he was only drawn in deeper.

Was he ready for that?

Then Kate reached down between their bodies, grasped him in her hand, and guided him towards her.

Sweet holy Christ.

It didn't matter if he was ready. He couldn't stop now to save his life.

He slid inside her with one thrust, and she arched her head back and cried out.

He braced his forearm against the wall and leaned in to press a quick, hard kiss onto her lips. He kept his other hand under her thigh, tightening his grip as he withdrew and slid back in.

Another slow stroke, and another. Kate's hands fisted in his shirt. Then he was pounding into her with hard, urgent thrusts, her soft cries driving him out of his mind.

He knew she was close when her body tightened around him. He reached down to roll her clit between his fingers, and then she was calling out his name as her head thrashed from side to side.

His own orgasm slammed into him like a tidal wave. He was gripped by ecstasy, shuddering and throbbing inside her.

After what seemed like a long time, he realized he was pressing kisses against her throat and murmuring her name like a prayer.

He wanted to stay inside her forever. But when their breathing finally slowed, he gently disengaged their bodies.

He searched her face for some sign of what she was feeling, but her eyes were closed. Then she gave a long, low sigh.

"That was incredible," she murmured.

His heart tightened in his chest.

"You're incredible," he whispered. "And we're incredible together."

She opened her eyes. "Sexually, yes."

He shook his head. "Not just sexually. That's not all I want from you."

She took in a deep breath and let it out. "Oh, Ian . . . you don't know what you want. And I'm not going to be your emotional punching bag while you figure it out."

There was finality in her voice, and it was like a knife in his chest. He wanted to argue with her, to tell her he did know what he wanted. But how could he? He hadn't given her any reason to trust him. She had too much reason to be gun-shy where he was concerned.

"That's fair enough," he said. "But someday—"

She shook her head. "No. That door is closed. The fact that we had sex doesn't change anything between us."

There was a pause, and then her voice softened a little. "It's not like we'll never see each other again. I'll still be spending time with Jacob."

"Sure," he said, striving to sound reasonable.

"Would you like me to pick him up on Friday?"

"Sure."

"Okay, then. Friday it is."

She looked down as she tugged her skirt into place and ran her hands through her hair. "Take care until then."

His cue to go. He straightened his clothes, grabbed his overcoat from the floor, and headed for the door.

He looked back at her for a second, wishing he had her gift for expressing feelings. If he did, he'd say something now that would explain the pain and confusion and longing churning inside him. Something that would fix everything between them.

But he didn't have her way with words. So he'd just have to earn her trust with his actions.

And the first action he could take was to respect her obvious desire to get rid of him right now.

"You take care, too," he said, his hand on the knob.

"I will," she said softly.

And that was that.

Chapter Twelve

Thursday's tea had turned into a movie and drinks with Simone, Maria, and Vicki. When Kate had rolled into bed at 3:00 a.m., she'd been planning to sleep in till noon the next day.

But an insistent buzzing woke her up earlier than that. She cracked open an eye, realized it was her cell phone, and glanced at the clock.

It was 11:00 a.m. She might feel like death on a cracker, but it was a perfectly reasonable hour for a call. She looked at her phone and saw Ian's name on the screen.

As usual, thoughts of him led to thoughts of his hand under her thigh, holding her in place as he thrust inside her.

She shivered.

But she'd had a week of practice at quelling those memories, and now she lay back on her pillow and answered his call.

"Hi, Ian."

"Have you seen Jacob today? Has he been in touch with you?"

Kate sat straight up in bed. "No, of course not. Why are you—"

"He's gone," Ian said, his voice cracking.

For a moment she couldn't take it in. "What do you mean, gone?"

"I mean he's gone. As in nobody knows where he is."

Her hand tightened on the phone. "My God. What happened?"

"The school had a field trip today—I signed the permission slip a week ago and dropped him off this morning. The buses were all lined up. A little while later, I got an automated message from the school informing me that Jacob was absent. I've gotten those before, when he's been out sick—it's the school's way of confirming that the parents know about the absence. I assumed it was a mistake and called the school. It wasn't a mistake. He never got on his bus. He must have waited until my car was out of sight and then taken off."

"You don't think he was . . ." She couldn't bring herself to say the word *kidnapped*.

"No, thank God. The police already checked the security footage from in front of the school, and they saw him leaving on his own. He was heading south, but of course that doesn't mean anything. He could be anywhere by now. We tried the GPS on his phone, but he didn't take it with him. He left it at the apartment."

"Oh, Ian. Where are you now? Are you at home?"

"No. I couldn't sit still and do nothing. I asked a friend to stay at the apartment in case Jacob calls there or comes home, but I had to go out and look for him. I'm in my car right now." He hesitated. "Can I come get you, Kate? Will you . . . will you look for him with me?"

"Of course," she said immediately. She'd never heard Ian sound like this before—scared, frantic, vulnerable. And when she thought about Jacob, wandering alone through the city, she was scared, too.

She threw on some clothes and went downstairs to wait. She was out on the sidewalk when Ian pulled up in his own car—a dark green Jaguar. She pulled open the passenger door and slid in beside him.

He'd changed out of his work clothes into jeans and a tee shirt. Every muscle in his body was tense, and his hands gripped the steering wheel so hard his knuckles were white.

"Thank you" was all he said as he started to pull away from the curb.

"Wait," she said, putting a hand on one of his. "Do you know where you're going, or are you just driving around?"

"Just driving around," he said, his voice miserable.

"Then let's talk about this for a minute. Did something happen? Can you think of a reason Jacob would run away?"

Ian rubbed his face with his hands. "He was pretty mad at me about . . . about what happened with you. But I thought he'd forgiven me for that. He knows I apologized to you, and . . . he seemed okay last night and this morning." His voice turned bitter. "Not that I'm the best judge."

"That's probably not it, then. Is there anything else? A problem at school, something he wanted to avoid?"

A sudden spasm of pain twisted his face. "There is one thing. But I don't see why Jacob would run away because of it."

"What is it?"

"His mother died a year ago. A year ago tomorrow."

Her heart clenched in her chest. "Oh, Ian." Then, suddenly, she remembered something. "Wait a minute. Did you read Jacob's story? The comic book he wrote?"

Ian nodded.

"Do you remember the character of the teenage boy? Simon?"

"Yeah."

"Simon lost both his parents in a car accident. Do you remember what he did before he went to the magician to get his power?"

Ian stared at her, his eyes widening. "He went to visit his parents' graves."

"Right."

"Oh my God." Ian took his hands from the steering wheel to cover his face. After a moment he dropped them and took a deep breath.

"Tina is buried in a cemetery in White Plains. And it's not far from the train station. If he left from Grand Central, the trip would only take forty-five minutes."

This time when he put the car into gear, she didn't stop him.

They drove in silence for half an hour. Ian navigated the route with the intense focus of a race-car driver, and all Kate could do was grab the handle above the passenger door and hold on.

Once they got off the Cross-Westchester Expressway they slowed down a little, and it wasn't long before they arrived at a sprawling cemetery.

Ian parked on the street, and he and Kate went through the iron gate and started to walk along the main path. Ian didn't say anything. He moved fast, and Kate concentrated on keeping up.

The tension that rolled off him in waves was a sharp contrast with their surroundings. Everything was lush and green and peaceful. A gentle breeze stirred the leaves on the trees, and the path they walked on was a mosaic of sun and shadow.

After about five minutes, Ian stopped and Kate followed the direction of his gaze.

Jacob was twenty yards away, sitting on the grass in front of a marble gravestone. His back was to them. His arms were wrapped around his shins and his head was on his knees, and he looked small, forlorn, and very young.

Kate turned to look at Ian, and she was shocked to see that his face was wet with tears.

"He's okay," he said brokenly.

Kate put an arm around his waist and gave him a quick, hard hug. "I'll wait for you back at the car."

He jerked his head around to look at her. "You're not coming with me?"

She shook her head. "The two of you need a chance to talk things over."

His mouth twisted. "So I can make everything better?"

"Ian—"

He cut her off. "There's not a relationship in my life I haven't screwed up. You know that as well as anyone. I'm starting to think . . ."

He paused. "Jacob's grandparents offered to take him in after Tina died. But she named me guardian in her will, and I wanted . . . I was determined to justify her trust. Now I wish I'd taken them up on their offer." He paused again. "But it's not too late. It's obvious I'm not a fit guardian. It's time I turn the job over to someone who is."

"Ian, look at me."

He did. His eyes were tormented and his jaw was tight, and every line in his face told the story of the pain he was feeling.

"Can I tell you something my grandmother used to say? Or would that be annoying?"

He actually smiled a little. "No. Go ahead and tell me."

"There are only two things in life you can't change—yesterday and tomorrow. But there's nothing you can't do today."

She looked him in the eyes. "You don't have to have all the answers when you talk to Jacob. You don't have to have *any* answers. All you have to do is love him—and be yourself." She laid a hand against his breastbone, right over his heart. "Your real self."

He looked down at her for a long moment. Then he nodded.

"Okay," he said quietly. "I'll try."

He turned and walked across the grass towards Jacob. Kate watched him for a moment, her heart aching for him—for both of them. Then she headed back to the car.

∼

Ian didn't say anything as he came up behind his nephew, but Jacob must have heard his footsteps. He twisted his head around, and when he saw his uncle standing there, his eyes widened.

Neither of them said anything for a minute. Then:

"Hey," Ian said.

"Hey."

There was an awkward pause.

"Are you mad at me?" Jacob asked after a long moment.

"No."

Jacob had been looking down, but now he met his uncle's eyes again.

Ian sat down on the grass next to him. "I was pretty scared, though," he said.

Jacob bit his lip. "I'm sorry."

"That's okay."

The two of them sat in silence for a few minutes, looking at Tina's gravestone.

BELOVED MOTHER, BELOVED SISTER, BELOVED FRIEND.

It occurred to Ian that there were worse ways to be remembered.

It also occurred to him that during the past year, he'd avoided talking about Tina to Jacob. He'd told himself he was respecting the boy's grief by giving him privacy, and that Jacob knew his uncle was available if he ever wanted to talk.

But his avoidance hadn't been about Jacob's pain. It had been about his own.

Jacob was doing his best to deal with his grief and loss. The fact that he was here proved that.

Ian was the one who hadn't been dealing with it.

Now, for the first time, he thought about his sister without jerking away from the memories as though they might burn him. He thought of her quick, sideways grin and the sparkle of mischief in her eyes. He thought of how proud he'd always been of her, how much he'd worried when she was overseas, how beautiful she'd looked on her wedding day, and how she'd struggled to keep it together at Joe's funeral.

He remembered meeting his nephew for the first time, a tiny wrinkled thing in his mother's arms. He remembered Tina smiling at a photo of Joe and hearing her whisper, "We did good, sweetheart."

He delved further back, to their childhood in Brooklyn and the Bronx. And then he remembered something he hadn't thought about in years.

"Did you know your mother loved to draw when she was your age?"

Jacob looked at him in surprise. "She did?"

Ian nodded. "Yeah. She had this sketchbook she carried with her everywhere, and for a long time she wouldn't let anyone see her drawings. I think she was in fifth grade when she showed them to me for the first time. They were good."

"I didn't know she liked to draw."

"You're a lot like your mom, you know."

"I am?"

"Yeah."

Jacob rested his chin on his knees. "I never thought I was anything like her. She was so strong and brave."

"You're strong and brave, too."

"No, I'm not."

"Yes, you are. If you weren't, you wouldn't have finished your book. It takes strength and courage to create something—especially when it seems like no one in your life believes in you. But you didn't give up. You believed in yourself. Your mother would be so proud of you, Jacob. Just like I am."

Jacob hugged his knees tighter. "Thanks," he said.

They were quiet after that. As they sat in the gentle stillness of the cemetery, Ian felt something inside him loosen—the hard bitterness of pain he'd never been able to acknowledge or release.

"Jacob," he said after a while. "If I ask you a question, will you give me an honest answer? Even if you think it might hurt my feelings?"

His nephew nodded. "Okay."

"Do you want to keep living with me? Or would you rather live with your grandparents?"

There was a short silence—but it was long enough for Ian to realize what he wanted the answer to be.

Jacob's lip trembled. "I want . . . I want . . ." He stopped. "Can I really tell you what I want?"

He was going to say he wanted to live with his grandparents. Steeling himself against the pain, Ian nodded. "You can tell me anything."

"I want my cat. And I don't want to play football, or soccer, or basketball."

A rush of emotion left Ian feeling weak. "You don't have to."

"I was thinking, though . . . baseball might not be so bad."

Ian laughed a little shakily. "Well, then, that's something we can talk about."

"But what about Remeow? Your building doesn't allow pets."

Your building, he'd said. Not *our* building.

"Then we'll move."

Jacob stared at him. "Do you really mean it?"

"Yes."

Jacob blinked behind his glasses. Then he threw his arms around his uncle, and Ian hugged him back with everything he had.

∽

They walked back to the car soon afterwards. Jacob was happy to see Kate, although he was embarrassed that she'd come out to White Plains to look for him.

His plan, he told them, had been to take the train back to Manhattan, head for the museum where the school had gone for its field trip, and rejoin his class. He'd been hoping with eleven-year-old optimism that no one would notice he was gone.

"I didn't mean to worry you guys. Honest."

He looked even guiltier when he heard Ian making phone calls—to the police, to the school, and to the friends he'd enlisted to help in the search.

Finally Ian slid the phone back in his pocket and turned to look at his nephew. "Why didn't you ask me to bring you here, Jacob? I would have."

Jacob looked down at his sneakers. "I know, but . . . I kind of wanted to be alone with my mom." He flushed. "I guess that sounds stupid."

"No," Ian said gently. "It doesn't sound stupid."

Jacob looked up again. "Maybe next time, though, we could go together."

Ian felt tears stinging the insides of his eyelids. "I'd like that," he said.

They drove to Jacob's old neighborhood, stopping at the house of the neighbors who'd taken in Remeow. The big orange feline was lounging on the porch, and Ian, who'd been afraid he might not remember Jacob after a year, was astonished when the cat came to meet the boy like an old friend, twining around his ankles and arching his head up for petting.

"You're really going to move to a new apartment just so Jacob can have his cat?"

When he looked at Kate, she was grinning at him.

"Yes. Do you think that's crazy?"

She shook her head. "I think it's wonderful."

"Considering the source, I don't find that reassuring."

Kate smacked him lightly on the arm and turned to greet Mrs. Burton, who'd just come out of the house. The woman had a friendly hello for the two of them and a huge hug for Jacob, who settled down on the porch swing with Remeow in his lap while the adults went inside the house.

Ian gave Mrs. Burton a brief summary of the day's events, finishing with his intention to bring Remeow to Manhattan as soon as he found a new apartment.

"Well, I won't deny that I'll miss him—but I'm delighted that he and Jacob will be reunited. I've never known a boy kinder to animals than your nephew. He has a good heart."

Ian nodded. "He does."

"You know," Kate put in, "Remeow could stay with me while you're apartment hunting. That way Jacob could visit him."

"Gallifrey wouldn't mind?"

"Oh, he'll mind. But he'll deal with it."

"Well . . ." He glanced at Mrs. Burton. "Would it be all right if we took Remeow home with us today?"

The dark-haired woman nodded. "Of course. Although . . ." She hesitated. "My husband was looking forward to seeing Jacob, after he called this morning to ask if he could come for a visit. We didn't realize he was away without leave," she added with a wry smile. "We both dearly love that boy, you know. We watched him for Tina from the time he was a baby."

Ian nodded. "My sister loved you like family."

Tears sprang to Mrs. Burton's eyes. "Thank you." She wiped her eyes, gave a quick sigh, and then smiled. "I tell you what. You probably want to get him home as soon as you can, after the stressful day you've had. But we'd love to have Jacob stay with us tonight. We talked about having him over all last year, but nothing ever came of it."

Ian had been aware of the standing invitation, but, given the monthly visits to his grandparents that already disrupted Jacob's schedule, he'd thought it would be better for his nephew to be home the rest of the time. Now he wished he'd reached out to Mrs. Burton sooner.

"Let me go talk to Jacob," he said.

An hour later, having had tea and cookies and met Mr. Burton, Ian was driving south on the Saw Mill Parkway with Kate in the passenger seat. They'd been invited to breakfast the next morning with the Burtons, after which they would take Jacob—and Remeow—back to Manhattan.

It was a quiet drive. Ian's heart was too full for him to be able to say much. Every so often he glanced at Kate, who was looking thoughtful beside him.

Something had happened to him in that cemetery. It was as though everything inside him had shaken loose from its moorings. And after the dust had settled, all his priorities had shifted.

Things that had once seemed important no longer did. And things he'd once believed he could live without, he now knew he couldn't.

He pulled up in front of Kate's building, and the two of them sat in silence for a moment.

He was the one to break it.

"If your answer is no, I'll understand. But is there a chance you'd consider coming home with me tonight? Not to sleep with me—just to stay with me. I have two guest rooms, and you can have your pick."

Kate looked at him. "I will if that's what you want. But why don't you stay here instead? I have a guest room, too. And I'm ten minutes closer to White Plains," she added with a smile.

A wave of gratitude filled him. "I'd love to stay here. Thanks, Kate."

She directed him to the nearest garage, and a little while later the two of them were sitting in Kate's living room.

They talked about Jacob, and Tina, and Kate's three brothers. They talked about music and their favorite movies. They talked about *Powers*, and which actors they thought should voice the different characters.

Kate informed him that he should start getting more comfortable with cats, and as a first step she put Gallifrey in his lap and showed him how he liked to be petted.

At first he just put up with it. But after a while, as Gallifrey settled down and began to purr, he actually started to enjoy it.

"You know, there *is* something kind of comforting about having a cat on your lap," he mused.

Kate nodded smugly. "There's a scientific basis for that. Cats purr within a range of twenty to a hundred and forty hertz, which has proven therapeutic benefits, from lowering blood pressure to promoting bone strength."

It was at that moment that Ian knew the truth.

He was in love with Kate Meredith.

As he sat there looking at her, it occurred to him that for the rest of his life he'd never be able to forget that cats purr within a range of 20 to 140 hertz.

There was nothing explosive or earth-shattering about the realization. It came gently, softly, almost invisibly.

But it changed everything.

Someday soon, he was going to tell her. But first he wanted a chance to show her that he was a man worth loving.

So when they realized it had gotten late, he didn't give in to the urge to sweep her into his arms and kiss her senseless. Instead he followed her down the hall to the guest room, thanked her for the spare toothbrush and towels, and said good night.

He shucked his clothes and slid naked between the clean-smelling sheets. Everything in this room made him think of Kate—the comfortable cleanliness, the mix of antique and modern furniture, the pictures on the walls and the books on the shelves.

He fell asleep with a smile on his face.

Chapter Thirteen

Kate lay awake for a long time, staring up at the ceiling. It had happened while Ian was walking across the grass towards Jacob. She'd known exactly how he felt—how much he wanted to say the perfect thing to his nephew, and how certain he was that whatever he said would be the wrong thing.

But she didn't just know how he was feeling. She knew *him*.

And she loved him.

She shifted restlessly in bed, curling up on her side with her hands tucked under her chin.

The thought of telling Ian how she felt seemed impossible. She knew she loved him, but nothing else had changed. He was still himself, commitment-shy and emotionally unavailable.

And she was still herself.

She might be more emotionally mature than Ian, but that wasn't saying much.

She'd been with Chris for the wrong reasons. She'd been with him because it was easy and comfortable and predictable. Not exciting, not challenging, not exhilarating—just simple.

Being with Ian would never be simple.

She wasn't ready for that—and God knew Ian wasn't. But right now he was sleeping in her guest bedroom after a day that had wrung his heart and wiped him out emotionally.

And she wanted to comfort him. To be with him.

It would only be for one night, but she could live with that. As her grandmother had always said, right now is all we ever have.

She got out of bed and shed her pajamas. Then, naked, she went down the hall and opened Ian's door.

He was asleep.

For a minute she just looked at him, a smile tugging at the corners of her mouth. God, he was beautiful. Big and broad and strong and the sexiest man she'd ever known.

She went over to his bed and slid under the covers. She pressed her body to his, realizing immediately that he was naked, too.

He stirred and woke.

"Kate?" he said, his voice blurry with sleep. "Is this a dream?"

A sudden spasm of affection squeezed her heart.

"No," she murmured, letting her hand trail down his body. "I just realized there's something I didn't get to do the last time you were here."

She found his shaft and closed her fingers around it.

"Oh yeah?" he said hoarsely, his hands fisting in the sheets. "What's that?"

"I want to make you come with my mouth."

He hardened against her palm with a low moan. "Okay, now I *know* this is a dream."

She smiled at him, and then she slid down the bed and swirled her tongue over his hot, hard, throbbing flesh.

Ian groaned.

Kate took her time, enjoying the feel and taste of him—and the intense pleasure of driving him crazy. Before long he was twisting his hips and pushing himself into her, growling out her name and sliding one hand into her hair. She rode the waves of his desire to culmination, swallowing down the essence that spilled into her mouth and licking him gently as he came down from his orgasm.

"Come here," he said at the end of a long, satisfied sigh.

He spread his arms and she scooted up the bed, snuggling against his side as he stroked her hair.

"That was incredible," he murmured. "What did I do to deserve it?"

She put her arm around him. "Nothing. I did that for me, not for you."

He smiled. "I see. Well, then—I think the next thing we do should be for me."

A shiver of anticipation went through her.

"What did you have in mind?"

He shifted onto his side. "The last time I was here, you told me you don't let men go down on you. Is that still your policy?"

Her heart was pounding, but she just rolled onto her back and gazed up at the ceiling. "Well . . . I suppose it would only be fair to make an exception for you. After all, you've had a hard day. And you did let me go down on you."

"Mmmm" was all he said.

Then he was between her legs.

She squeaked, and then she moaned.

The next several minutes passed in a haze of pleasure. When she came it seemed to go on forever, her nerve endings lighting up like the Fourth of July.

Ian kissed his way back up her body and lay beside her, putting an arm around her waist and holding her close. In a few minutes they were asleep.

They woke up in the middle of the night, making love. Kate wasn't conscious of the transition; she knew only that one minute she was sleeping and the next she was on her back with Ian above her.

When he stroked his arousal against her heat, she gasped and threw her legs wide.

His eyes burned into hers. "You're sure about the pill? You're okay using just that?"

"Yes. And I'm clean. You?"

"Had a physical three months ago, and I haven't been with anyone but you since."

"Then for God's sake—"

He kissed her hard as he thrust inside her.

They went slow this time, drawing it out. She was hungry for him to the point of desperation, but she didn't want it to end, and Ian seemed to feel the same way.

His climax followed just after hers, and when the aftershocks subsided, Ian rolled to his side and pulled her against his chest.

God, she loved it there. Surrounded by Ian's big, warm body, she'd never felt so safe and so wild at the same time.

It was a wonderful combination.

She closed her eyes, figuring they'd fall asleep again. But after a minute Ian pulled back, and when she opened her eyes he was looking at her very seriously.

"There's something I have to tell you."

"All right," she said gently, knowing what was coming.

He was going to tell her that while tonight had been wonderful, he wasn't ready for more. And then she'd tell him she felt the same way.

"Kate, I love you."

For a moment the words didn't register. When they did, she blinked.

Okay, not what she'd expected. But she still knew what to do.

She kissed him softly and took his face between her hands.

"That's a very sweet thing to say, Ian. Really. But don't worry . . . I won't hold you to it in the morning."

He frowned. "But I want you to hold me to it."

She shook her head and smiled. "Let's get some sleep now, okay? We need to be on the road by eight thirty tomorrow."

"But—"

"Shh," she said, kissing him again.

He looked like he wanted to argue with her. Then he sighed and pulled her against him.

Kate, I love you.

For an instant after he'd said those words, her heart had soared—until she'd ruthlessly sent it back to her chest, where it belonged.

Ian was not a long-haul guy and probably never would be.

But even though nothing would come of it, she would treasure that moment forever.

∼

He hadn't said "I love you" to a woman since Paula, but it hadn't been hard, or terrifying, or any of the things he'd always thought it would be. Saying those words to Kate had been the easiest thing he'd ever done.

Now all he had to do was convince her he actually meant them.

Later that evening, after he and Jacob had settled Remeow at Kate's and gone back to their apartment, it occurred to Ian that he had access to someone who might be able to help him with his problem.

"Jacob, I need your advice."

"*My* advice? Sure."

They'd had Chinese for dinner and were eating brownies for dessert. Ian led the way into the living room and sat down across from his nephew.

"Okay, so . . . here's the thing." He took a deep breath. "I'm in love with Kate, and I want her to go out with me."

Jacob's eyebrows rose to his hairline. "You're in love with *Kate*?"

He sounded so surprised that Ian wondered if he disapproved. Maybe he even had a crush on her, or something like that.

"Um, yeah. Are you okay with that?"

"Okay with it? Of course I am! It just seems like, you know . . . you guys fight a lot. And I know you apologized, but you were really mean to her about that whole—"

"I know."

"I just don't want you to get your hopes up," Jacob went on, sounding like a concerned older brother instead of his eleven-year-old nephew. "I mean, Kate might not feel that way about you."

No kidding.

"I know that," he said. "But I have to give it my best shot, you know?"

Jacob nodded solemnly.

"So that's why I need your advice. I need a romantic way to tell her. You've gotten to know Kate pretty well in the last month, and you're creative like she is. I thought you might have some ideas."

"Hmm," Jacob said thoughtfully. "Well . . . I think the best thing you could do is make it into a story for her."

"A story?"

"Sure. Kate loves stories. And she thinks they're important."

"Important? What do you mean?"

"Kate says that without stories, reality would destroy us. She says stories and myths and heroes challenge us to be worthy of a larger reality. To listen to the better angels of our nature. To be more than what we are."

A sudden rush of goose bumps swept over his skin.

"Kate says that, huh?"

Jacob nodded.

Ian sat back in his chair. "Well, kid, I think you've got something there."

"I just thought of something else."

"Yeah?"

"Next weekend is her friend's wedding."

He was right—Saturday was the twelfth. "I'd forgotten all about it."

"Weddings are really romantic, right? You should tell her then. At the wedding. If you're going with her."

Was he going with her? He supposed the first thing to do was find out the answer to that question.

"Thanks, Jacob. You've been a big help."

He gave her a call that night. "Kate?"

"Hey, Ian. How's Jacob?"

"Doing well, I think. He's looking forward to seeing you on Tuesday." He paused. "He also reminded me that next weekend is Jessica's wedding."

He heard her gusty sigh over the phone. "Yes, it is. God help me."

"I was just wondering . . . do you still need a date?"

A short silence. "Well . . . I guess I do. Sure. That would be nice."

"You also mentioned something about the rehearsal dinner."

"That's on Friday night."

"I'd like to escort you to that, too."

Another pause. "Jessica did ask us to confirm by tomorrow if we're bringing dates, so she can give the restaurant the final head count."

"So how about it?"

"You really want to put yourself through this? There'll be toasts and speeches and a lot of obnoxious people."

"Which restaurant is it at?"

"Ludano's, on the Upper East Side."

"Then the food will make up for the speeches."

He heard her laugh. "Okay, then, you're on. Pick me up at six thirty."

"I'll be there."

And he would. He sure as hell would.

Chapter Fourteen

Kate couldn't help feeling a little flutter of anticipation as she got ready for the rehearsal dinner. Of course, this wasn't a date—after their night together the previous week, she and Ian had gone back to a friendship dynamic, which was definitely the best thing for both of them.

Sure, she felt a twinge of disappointment every now and then. That was only natural—just as it was natural to feel that electric rush of attraction every time she saw him. It wasn't as if her female hormones had stopped functioning just because her mind was being sensible.

And she didn't regret their last night together.

She decided she had no reason to feel self-conscious about making an effort with her appearance tonight. It was Jessica's rehearsal dinner, after all. Everyone would be dressed up.

The fact that Ian was her escort for the evening was only a secondary factor. And he definitely wasn't the reason she'd begged Simone to go shopping with her yesterday.

If it hadn't been for Simone, Kate would never have considered buying the dress she wore now. She slipped on the strappy sandals she'd bought to go with it and went to stand in front of the mirror.

The dress was sapphire blue—to match her eyes, Simone had explained. It was a simple design, with cap sleeves and a sweetheart neckline and a skirt that swirled around her knees in floating layers of silk tulle.

She loved it.

The intercom buzzed, and her flutter of anticipation turned into a riptide.

"There's a gentleman here for you," Andreas said. "Shall I send him up?"

"No, tell him I'll be right down," she answered.

She checked her hair once more in the mirror—she'd worn it in an upsweep, which actually made her neck seem long and elegant—and then grabbed her purse. A minute later, the elevator doors opened and she stepped out into the lobby.

As Andreas held the front door for her, she noticed a vintage Rolls-Royce at the curb.

"Wow. Whose car is that?"

He grinned at her. "I believe it's yours—at least for tonight."

Just then, the driver's side door opened and Ian emerged.

She blinked.

He complemented the car perfectly, even though he wasn't wearing anything vintage. He also wasn't in one of the business suits he wore to work, and he wasn't dressed as Spike.

His suit was modern and sexy and exquisitely tailored for his broad shoulders, and Kate had to resist the urge to fan herself.

"You really outdid yourself, Hart," she said, trying not to show how touched she was that he'd gone to all this trouble.

"And you look like a princess," he said, handing her a white rose she hadn't even noticed he was carrying.

She looked down at it to hide her sudden blush. "It's lovely. Thank you."

She glanced over her shoulder and saw that Andreas had gone back inside the lobby. Then she turned back to Ian, who was smiling at her.

"So . . . what's the deal with all this?" she asked cautiously. "It's wonderful, but a little over the top, don't you think?"

"I needed the right setting," he told her, leaning back against the gleaming white car and sliding his hands into the pockets of his dark gray suit.

"The right setting for what?"

"For a story I'd like to tell you."

A story?

"Well . . ." She hesitated. "I guess we have some time before we have to be at the restaurant. Is it a long story?"

He shook his head. "No."

"Okay, then."

He took a deep breath, and then he began.

"Once upon a time, a lonely man fell in love with a beautiful woman. But he was proud and blind and afraid, and he didn't realize his true feelings."

Her heart knocked against her rib cage. She squeezed the rose stem in her hand, belatedly grateful that its thorns had been removed.

"But one day the man was faced with the loss of something precious. And he knew in that moment that what really mattered to him were the people he loved: his nephew, and his friends, and the woman who'd taught him that magic is real—and that love is real, too." He paused. "And that cats purr between twenty and a hundred and forty hertz."

She was caught between tears and laughter.

"Damn you, Ian Hart," she muttered, grabbing a tissue from her purse and swiping at her eyes.

"What is it?"

"I never wear makeup. I put some on tonight, and now you've made me cry."

She stuffed the tissue back in her purse. Ian took it from her, along with the rose, and set them on the hood of the car.

Then he reached for her hands. "Kate Meredith, I love you. I have some long-term plans I don't think you're ready to hear yet, so for now, I'll just ask you this: Will you be my girlfriend?"

She wanted to say yes.

"I . . ." Her mouth was dry. She tried again. "I . . ."

She shook her head. "Oh, Ian. I know I called you a coward, but . . . maybe I'm the real coward. My heroines are brave, but I'm not. I was with Chris because it was easy. And even though it didn't work out with him, I don't know if I can handle . . ." Her voice trailed off.

"Me?"

"Well, yes."

He squeezed her hands. "The thing about being a writer is that you get to be in control. The characters you create have to act exactly the way you want them to. Being with me won't be like that . . . and it won't be easy. I won't always do the things you want me to, or the things you wish I would. But I promise to love you with everything I've got." He looked into her eyes. "And you're not a coward. You feel scared right now, but that doesn't make you a coward. You're every bit as brave as any of your heroines. You just need to let your own life be your greatest story."

Let your own life be your greatest story.

Her skin prickled. All her life, Kate had poured every color of the rainbow into her writing—but she'd been content for her own life to be in black and white. Now, for the first time, a new possibility opened in front of her.

Being with Ian would challenge her on every level. It would take courage, love, and imagination.

Everything she valued most.

"For a guy who claims he's not creative, you sure have a way with words sometimes."

He lifted her hand and kissed it. "So what do you say, Kate? Will you come with me on this adventure?"

And then, all at once, her excitement was bigger than her fear.

"Yes," she said, and he pulled her into his arms.

His mouth slanted over hers, and she felt his kiss in her bones. When they finally came up for air, she told him, "Now you've messed up my lipstick, too."

He grinned at her and opened the passenger door of the Rolls. "I make no apologies for that. My lady, your carriage awaits."

She got into the car, and Ian handed her the rose and her purse with a courtly bow before coming around to the driver's side.

"You know, this is harder for me than it is for you," he said as he settled in next to her. "I've had to adjust all my ideas about the world."

"What do you mean?"

"I never knew life could be like a fairy tale."

Her heart threatened to overflow. "I have to adjust my ideas, too," she said.

"How?"

"I never knew life could be better than a fairy tale."

She could have sworn his eyes were brighter than usual.

"Are you crying, Hart? That's so sentimental."

"I'm not crying," he said. "The sun's in my eyes."

She kissed him on the cheek. "Hey, Ian?"

"Yes?"

"I love you, too."

ACKNOWLEDGMENTS

A huge thank-you to the entire team at Montlake, especially the wonderful Maria Gomez. I'm also indebted to Charlotte Herscher, editor extraordinaire, who helped make this book better.

ABOUT THE AUTHOR

Abigail Strom started writing stories at the age of seven and has never been able to stop. On her way to becoming a full-time writer, she earned a BA in English from Cornell University, as well as an MFA in dance from the University of Hawaii, and held a wide variety of jobs from dance teacher and choreographer to human resource manager. Now she works in her pajamas and lives in New England with her family, who are incredibly supportive of the hours she spends hunched over her computer.

You can visit her website at www.abigailstrom.com or e-mail her at abigail@abigailstrom.com. She would love to hear from you!